SOLDIER ON

THE JOURNEY OF A WARRIOR

Meenakshi Nath Sharma

Wordly Wise Publishers

Published by
Wordly Wise Publishers & Distributors
3rd Floor, 44, Regal Building,
Hanuman Road Area, Connaught Place,
New Delhi 110001
+91-9836325999

Email – hello@wordlywise.co.in

ISBN : 978-93-94075-48-1

First impression (2024)

SOLDIER ON

THE JOURNEY OF A WARRIOR

Wordly Wise Publishers

Contents

Acknowledgement

I am starting from the very beginning by acknowledging those who inspired me to write and then made sure my dreams were fulfilled - Papa and Mummy, this is dedicated to both of you!

My husband, Captain (Indian Navy) Rikeesh Sharma, Veteran and a second generation *Fauji* has always given invaluable feedback. Our sons, Lt Cdr Rishabh Sharma, Sarthak Sharma and daughter-in-law, Ishita - thank you for being my cheerleaders.

Thank you, Ritu Didi for being a fountainhead of memory and wisdom with your guidance on timelines, people and places. Thank you to my nephews, Parv and Punya. Punya, it is your photograph of *Nanaji* that inspired the cover design of *Soldier On*.

Special thanks to *Taiji* Brij Aunty and *Mamiji* Shobha Aunty for their anecdotal references that added an extra element to the book.

Heartfelt gratitude to the Sikh Regiment for their wholesome support system while Papa was in service, as a veteran and for ensuring that he got a well-deserved final journey.

On behalf of Papa, I want to thank DLF Chairman K.P Singh for giving him an opportunity post retirement and for trusting him for almost three decades.

To all of Papa's course mates, friends and their families, especially Saroj Chopra Aunty for unstinting love.

Thank you to GLiterArti Book Club and their members for their encouragement.

Thank you to Sanjoy Roy, an inspirational boss, the man behind Jaipur Literature Festival, for inspiring so many of us to turn author.

Chandni Mathur, CEO of Wordlywise publisher has truly been a blessing as much as Sarah, my dear editor.

This has been a very fulfilling journey and I am thankful to have taken the first step with Soldier On.

Meenakshi Sharma
Gurgaon

Author's Note

The Soldier's heart, the Soldier's spirit, the Soldier's soul, are everything.

Nothing lasts forever, not even memories. It is all too easy to lose those precious stories unless we preserve them. This realization dawns when it is time to bid goodbye to loved ones.

Being one of the progenies does not make it any easier to document a rich past. What helps is the bonding that goes beyond filial duties. I imbibed the family values of my mother and struck an intellectual chord with my dad. While the former inspired me to practice gratitude, the latter pushed me to take on challenges much beyond what I thought possible. And then there was the work that turned out to be the mighty unifier. It began with our role as Directors of a firm and then our common interests kept us engaged as we expanded our partnership to the book club, a Literary Festival, running a magazine, and even steering real estate training and events. We did not always agree on issues, but we overcame all odds to collaborate in the most creative ways.

Just as coming events cast their shadow, the pandemic and its forced isolation became a preparation for an impending separation. It also gave wings to the long dormant dream of the book that you now hold in your hands.

What began as a difficult conversation turned into a shared project culminating in the precious discovery of handwritten notes that he thoughtfully left behind. Thus, came together a tale that harked back to the 18th Century, navigated the tumultuous pre-partition era and reached its conclusion during an unprecedented pandemic.

Destiny failed to extinguish that smouldering ember that was passed on to me like an Olympic torch. And yet, every time I felt cheated at being left to pick up those scraps, I was reminded of those who never gave up, whatever the odds! And this is what has inspired me to tell the tale that must be told.

'Soldier On' is not just the story of a brave officer of the Indian Armed Forces and that of a stoic family, but a saga of love and loss, courage and hope and the fragility and vulnerability of every family that struggles to reconcile the old-world values of bravery and steadfastness with the complexities of modern life.

Prologue

'Papa, we are now turning into your lane. Are you ready to leave?'

This was a standard opening line every time we made our way to his house to pick him up to attend an event. In this case, the monthly GLiterARti book club meetup at the DLF City Club in Gurgaon.

'I am ready and waiting for you,' would be his response, even when he was far from ready. Today was an exception. I spotted him even before the call disconnected. There he was, my dear father, a comfortingly familiar figure, standing ramrod straight, and his hand resting protectively over a leather bag strung across his body.

I was a child again, looking for my father as school got over on those rare days when he was in town. The only difference from then to now was the shiny bald pate – what he laughingly referred to as proof of his brilliant mind. Only now, he had begun to cover it up. This recent transformation into a fashionista meant I would be left guessing his headgear. Would he be sporting a beret, a cowboy style fedora or his Army style cap?

It turned out to be the latter in his favourite regimental colours, with his name 'Prithvi' proudly emblazoned on one side with the slogan '18 till I die' on the back. It suited him well, as did the impressive nameplate of his townhouse in the posh DLF locality. As the sole occupant of this house, he was a self-proclaimed 'King of the Castle' and he looked the part too.

He raised his hand in a signal to stop even as I did a double take and looked again. Was he wearing a tuxedo? The car halted and with his entry, I was enveloped by the heady fragrance of 'Old Spice' along with a wave of nostalgia that transported me to those good old days.

A shuffle, a sigh and a trademark *Hare Ram* were the only signs of advancing age as he took the time to glance at his *Ashram* (retreat) before raising his arm in farewell in the direction of his trusted attendant, Abdul, who lived in the outhouse with Saheeda. Once comfortable in his favoured spot, he beamed at the compliment from my husband.

'Looking sharp in this perfectly fitted Park Avenue suit.'

I primed myself to acknowledge him in the same way, without sounding judgemental.

'Papa, you look great...but why so formal? It is just a book club.'

He was offended.

'What do you mean? And it is not just a book club! This is the most happening book club of Gurgaon, where every member is an intellectual. Plus, today is special as it will be followed by high tea...hosted by me,' he finished with a flourish, like a magician pulling out a rabbit from his hat, reminding me just how much he loved drama, playing to the gallery and indulging in theatrics.

'People have forgotten the art of dressing, Rikki,' he then addressed my husband, proceeding to ignore me as only he could. And behind his spectacles, those light brown eyes that I inherited, twinkled with steely resolve.

'All I need is Tea and Sympathy,' he hummed gently, referring to the 1956 film while thumbing through 'The Night Circus' by Erin Morgenstern, the book which was up for discussions today. Silence prevailed for the next few minutes as he became deeply absorbed in this fantasy novel and then we pulled into the driveway of the City Club in DLF, Phase 4. My husband stopped at the porch to allow him to disembark before heading to the parking lot. I walked a few steps behind him into the luxurious Club lobby. The hint of lime and Earl Grey tea wafted languidly and while I was asked to show my membership card, he breezed in with panache-a long-term member with a close association with DLF, he exuded charisma.

'Hello, Colonel! Amazingly dressed as always,' called out a member.

He placed his right hand over his heart and smiled in acknowledgement as he continued walking into the lobby. His style and attitude were a mix of military correctness and corporate suave, which was truly a sight to behold.

The next few minutes were infused with the warmth of familiarity and common interests as book lovers exchanged pleasantries. Amidst critical commentaries and analysis, when it was his turn to review the book, he waxed eloquent about the book and himself. Recalling his love for reading, he began to reminisce. 'I borrowed 'Gone with the Wind' at the age of ten and memorized all of Shakespeare's plays before I was twelve.'

I had heard these stories before and believed each one of them; so irresistible was his energy and language skills. It had to be a divine gift unless one could attribute it to a sheer zest for life. He continued talking about himself as people listened. Some with admiration, others with amusement. Either way, we were inevitably transfixed with the energy and intensity.

'Be it the *Vedas* or the Song Divine, I had done it all by the time I turned 15 when I became a soldier and that changed my life.'

The admiration was now full-blown and well-deserved. I was still mulling over this thought of a young boy who loved to read being subjected to rigorous training in the National Defence Academy when I heard peals of laughter.

My dad was regaling the book club audience with the dramatic reading of a passage, his love for the written word evident in every nuance and every inflexion. His book review was incisive and inventive, whimsical, and imaginative, much like him. And as the reading concluded, he summed it up.

'This is a book which deserves to be read by everyone. It is real, it is romantic and it is truthful just like all of us - the intellectuals of Gurugram.'

The applause was heartfelt, as was the camaraderie. He was in his element, effortlessly integrating high praise for the book with an appreciation of this community of book lovers. And that wasn't all.

True to his word, he turned charming host, personally ensuring that the tea service was impeccable. This was everyone's favourite time when we relished a post-meeting treat. The one today was just another culinary delight replete with well-dressed servers who discreetly confirmed your choice of beverage, repeating the request and noiselessly pouring it while balancing the perfectly brewed concoction with hot milk in silver kettles. The ceremony was a treat for the eyes, a perfect harmony of actions that can only be experienced.

And it wasn't just that perfect tea cup with the perfect colour of tea or the warmth of those freshly baked cookies or delectable onion fritters that made it such a beautiful experience. It was about the amazing bond that we had built in the midst of a perfect setting. The joy of discussing the most eclectic subjects is what made us all feel alive as we debated and deliberated on any subject under the sun, free from any shackles or labels or moral policing. Time just flew and as it grew dark, we bid our goodbyes.

Not before Papa extended another invite. This time, it was 'At Home' for his homemade momos along with buckwheat crepes. The response to this invitation was enthusiastic. A date was set and a promise was made.

On our way back, that effervescence was missing. He was uncharacteristically silent, perhaps worn out from the effort that he was putting into being such a showman. I sensed that he was working extra hard to keep up the image of a vibrant and flamboyant veteran who still had the ability to charm everyone. It tugged at my heartstrings and I felt a surge of protective emotion. The contrasts between exuberance and loneliness were becoming all too obvious. More so when we pulled up in front of the house that my parents built, it had always been imposing and regal, but today, it seemed subdued, a pale shadow of its illustrious past. Overwhelmed by the grim realization that time and tide wait for none, I clutched at those memories of the past. And then I remembered what my father had said. 'It is my story and it is best narrated by me!'

Over to Papa!

I am the eternal one.

I am the universe.

I am Planet Prithvi.

Family Tree of Col Prithvi Nath, VSM

- Pandit Riga Misr
  - Misr Maha Bali *(Courtier, Maharaja Ranjit Singh)*
    - Uttam Chand
      - Nand Lal
      - Ram Lal
      - Ram Kishan
      - Jai Kishan
        - Salig Ram
        - Pandit Baij Nath
          - Ram Nath *(Member of the Order of the British Empire)*
          - Banwari Nath & Prem Kaur
            - Kaushalya
            - Narinder Nath
            - Pushpa
            - Santosh
            - Surinder Nath
            - Krishna
            - Col Prithvi Nath & Urmil Nath
              - Ritu Vats & Tanmaya Vats
                - Parv Vats
                - Punya Vats
              - Meenakshi Sharma *(Author)* & Capt Rikeesh Sharma (IN)
                - Lt Cdr Rishabh Sharma
                - Sarthak Sharma
              - Nalini
                - Neelesh
            - Rani
          - Vishwa Nath
          - Peshori Nath
          - Labh Chand
    - Beli Ram *(Treasurer , Maharaja Ranjit Singh and the caretaker of Kohinoor Diamond)*

1849
Punjab

He took a long, deep breath, savouring the heady aroma of roses intermingled with the earthy sweetness of *Raat ki Rani* (night jasmine), bringing back delightful memories of fragrant Delhi winters. Soft strains of the *Gurbani* (religious chants) floated in from Gurudwara Bangla Saheb, adding tranquillity to the magnificent serenity that imbued this misty winter morning with peaceful calm.

It was *Amrit Vela*, a time of meditation just before dawn, at Rouse Avenue, which merges into Baba Kharak Singh Marg. A young teenager walks around the park that borders the Government quarters with his middle-aged father. His heart is full, as are his pockets, with *chilgoze* (pine nuts) that his father picked up from the neighbourhood dry fruit shop. They serve as a reminder of their roots in Kabul in Afghanistan, the place from where his family came to India over two centuries ago.

These moments are deeply cherished because they have been squeezed from a busy schedule at the Viceroy and Governor General's house in close proximity to the now *Rashtrapati Bhavan.*

They saunter arm-in-arm, trying to beat the winter chill while delving into the past and looking into the future. As they head towards the lone wooden bench just outside the park, the anticipation is mixed with melancholy because I will soon be leaving this familiarity to embark on a brand-new journey.

'*Kaka*, you must never forget our ancestry,' *Bauji* spoke with emotion, calling me by the nickname that only he and my mother ever used.

'The *Kumarias* & the *Trikhas* who lived in Kabul for 250 years as courtiers and commanders of the Sikh Empire were originally the *Misrs*.'

'I know we use the surname *Kumaria's,* but who are the *Trikhas*? And how are they different or similar, *Bauji*?' I ask.

'As Punjabi Brahmins, we are part of the *Panchjati* (community of five), which also includes the *Jhingan, Jaitley* and the *Mohlas*. Your mother was the only sister of seven brothers or what was called '7 *Bharava Di Sat Bharavi Behen'*, the only sister of seven brothers. They belonged to the 'Silver Arm' *Trikhas*.'

'Silver Arm *Trikhas*,' I repeat incredulously. 'What does that even mean?'

'Your mother's great uncle's right arm was severed during a battle with the Mughals and it was his courage and loyalty that was commended when he was presented with a silver arm by none other than Sher-e-Punjab, Raja Ranjit Singh!'

My father paused to see the impact of this impromptu history lesson on me. I was wide-eyed and speechless because this was not the kind of story one could ignore. It was a revelation of some deep truths that were closely connected with both sides of my own family. While I vaguely recalled hearing this story in my childhood, I remember ignoring and dismissing it as an urban legend. But this time around, there was no mistaking its authenticity as my father corroborated the facts brick by brick.

'So, I am also a part of the '*Chandi Di Baanh Wale*' family of Raja Ranjit Singh's court?'

He smiled and obliged me by elaborating further.

'Maharaja Ranjit Singh, the Lion of Punjab, played an integral role not just in Punjab and Jammu and Kashmir but also in swathes of territory right up to Khyber Pass. In line with the teachings of Guru Gobind Singh, who believed in the combination of political power and spiritual equality, he did it through *Misrs*, combining regal power with spirituality. Our historically known lineage starts from our forefather, *Misr* Maha Bali, who was a courtier in Maharaja Ranjit Singh's *Darbar* (court). He had two sons, Uttam Chand*ji* and Beli Ram*ji*. Beli Ram*ji* became the treasurer of the *Toshakhana* (Treasury) of Raja Ranjit Singh and was by his side even when the *Maharaja* was on his deathbed. Our forefathers were the direct descendants of Pandit Uttam Chand, whose son Pandit Jai Kishan was my grandfather, so my great-granduncle was none other than Beli Ram, who played an integral role in history. Did you know that the Maharaja had pledged the Kohinoor, then known as *Syamantak Mani*, to Lord Jagannath of Odisha? The Maharaja refused to bow to the British and in keeping with this honourable tradition, neither did Beli Ram*ji*. And for that, he was severely punished.'

'But why didn't someone intervene? Didn't Raja Ranjit Singh have any heirs?'

'He did. But the British refused to accept Maharaja's son Kharak Singh or his grandson Naunihal Singh as his heirs. In fact, Beli Ram*ji* managed to anger Naunihal Singh for refusing to hand over the Kohinoor and was fined and imprisoned by him. Meanwhile, the British began pitching for his youngest

Queen, Rani Jindan Kaur, as the Queen. Rani Jindan was no pushover, but the British drove her into exile. She began fighting for the rights of her son Duleep Singh, who was forcibly taken away to London and converted to Christianity. In 1846, a gullible seven-year-old *Maharaja* Duleep Singh was forced to sign the Treaty of Lahore on behalf of the Sikhs, marking the end of the Anglo-Sikh war and our ownership of the Kohinoor which was handed over to Queen Victoria in 1850.'

A barrage of questions swirled in my head.

'So, what happened to Beli Ram*ji*?'

'He was tortured by the British for his refusal to hand over the Kohinoor for presentation to Queen Victoria after the Treaty of Lahore in 1849. It is not known whether he was murdered or escaped, but his fate was inextricably linked with this beautifully precious stone which brought nothing but bad luck upon him.'

He let out an audible sigh. This was an emotional interaction that had stoked his patriotic fervour. He gazed wistfully at the Indian flag fluttering in the distance and I wondered if his thoughts matched mine as I could hardly contain my excitement at the realization that my lineage was determining my career choice and the course of my life. I wanted to get to know my roots better.

'I know we are Punjabi Hindus who belong to Amritsar, but beyond that, I know nothing more as we have not spent too much time here. I would love to know more.'

I spoke straight to his heart. This was a topic that inevitably cheered him up. His face lit up and his eyes turned wistful.

'*Ambarsar,* true to its name, is a sacred pool of nectar. Every inch of it calls out to me. It is the seat of learning, a place of the Gurus. It is my home and home to the holy *Darbar*

Sahab or what the British called the Golden Temple. I have an equal amount of love for the Durgiana Mandir, a replica of the *Darbar Sahab*, where I served as trustee. More importantly, this is our *Karambhoomi*, the place where we have lived and worked and one which has benefited from the contributions of our family - my father and your grandfather.'

He wistfully recalled the days of glory as he walked down memory lane.

'Our family has always been serving the country and our community - as courtiers, as warriors, as priests or as educationists. Our upbringing and education have not just given us respect but also a huge responsibility. I mentioned how the brother of Beli Ram*ji*, Pandit Uttam Chand, was my great-grandfather, and Pandit Jai Kishan was my own grandfather. Then came the person whose name continues to make our family proud. His birth was fortuitous and changed the destiny of his blind and destitute mother. Can you guess who I am talking about?'

'Yes, of course. Are you referring to my grandfather and your father - Pandit Baij Nathji? Tell me about him, *Bauji*.'

I was eager to know more about the person who I never met as he passed away before I was born, but was a name that dominated our household conversations.

As the soft glow of the rising sun spread like fire across the skies, my father began narrating the achievements of his illustrious father.

'The great visionary, reformer and extraordinary educationist who built his life from scratch in Amritsar was my father. Stories tell us that he heard the heart-rending cries of a woman from inside the *Shamshan Ghat* (Cremation Ground) when he was returning late from school on horseback. Instead of panicking, this brave lad galloped into the dark recesses of the ground to find a woman tied to a tree. Once freed, she said she was falsely accused of witchcraft by the fanatics and left to die alone. Not one to believe in such horrifying superstitions, he respectfully restored her to her parents. This was just the beginning of his humanitarian efforts. He was meant for great things and as a reformer and educationist, he went on to establish the Pandit Baij Nath High School in 1887. He gave a fillip to education and to society while also emerging as the head of our *Panchjaati* (five castes).

'Sounds like an amazing man,' I murmured.

'He had the courage and he had the character. He also believed in the principles of modern education that were unheard of at that time. He advocated discipline and physical fitness through *Akharas* (wrestling grounds), swimming, cricket and even scouting. And he wasn't just an educationist. He was also a social reformer and humanitarian who would come to the aid of the underprivileged.'

He paused to let me take it all in, but I was itching for answers as the questions swirled in my head.

'*Bauji,* everyone in your family has such close ties with Amritsar. But we have only lived in Delhi and Shimla. Why is that?'

'That's another story that is worth recounting,' my father paused before continuing.

'You may call it divine providence, but during the horrific Jallianwala Bagh massacre in 1919, I was just a young boy who witnessed a slice of history. And what a massive tragedy that was. The pain, the cries, the anger, the hate…I can feel it crawl up on me even today. It did not end that day. Just a few days after the massacre, the local District Collector, Sir Miles Irving, was targeted by an angry mob. I happened to spot a group of rioters and raised an alarm. It was my warning that helped Sir

Miles to escape. I never planned any of it, and it happened because I observed the movement and felt I should report it.

As a reward, for protecting Sir Irving from mob lynching, my father was summoned to make an offer of a job for me at the Viceroy's office in Delhi. I was still studying, but my father encouraged me to take it up as it was a good opportunity. This is how I left Amritsar and became a Secretary at the Viceroy's office.'

The question tumbled out.

'Your parents or brothers? Did they not accompany you?'

'My father had by then established a chain of PBN Schools in English and Hindi medium and was deep into his work. My older brother Pandit Ram Nath assisted my father and his sons continue the legacy of Pandit Baij Nath High School till now. In fact, years later, Pandit Ram Nath was awarded the MBE (Member British Empire) title in 1928 for his continued contributions to education, which was recorded in the London Gazette. My younger brother, Pandit Vishwa Nath, a brilliant professor of Zoology, rose to be the Principal of Government College Lahore and joined the *Maharaja* of Patiala's cricket team. All of them were equally busy in their individual journeys, doing quite well for themselves.' *(Refer family tree)*

'So were you...you gave us the best life possible, even after my mother...your wife passed away...'

I felt a lump in my throat as I mentioned my mother's name. He took a second to recover before going back to his storytelling.

'I miss your mother too. Wouldn't you like to know how I met her?' his eyes twinkled at the recollection.

I nodded immediately, and he was always happy to talk about her.

'Your *Mamaji* (mother's elder brother) Gian Chand was

a Revenue Collector and had met Pandit Baij Nath in 1916. They were mutually impressed with each other's background and lineage and felt this would be a match made in heaven. So when the proposal came a few years later, my father readily accepted. By that time, I was employed in Delhi at the Viceroy's office and was 23 years old, while your mother, Prem Kaur, was barely 16. True to her name, she was beautiful, loving and courageous. Devoted to humanity, she believed in service with a smile. A true warrior, *Trikha*, with a deep sense of patriotism, she managed to support my career while also supporting the Indian National Movement. And, as you already know, she was a wonderful mother to all of you. And now she is your guardian angel, watching over you, giving you strength, my son.'

My father stood up and held my shoulders while he looked straight into my eyes.

'Loyalty, Discipline and Learning ... these are the values our family believes in. You are our 'Prithvi', our entire world and you are a true scholar soldier – a *Sant Sipahi* who must carry on the warrior and priest legacy. It is no mean task to clear the prestigious JSW (Joint Services Wing) exam on your own merit and now you will be joining the Indian Armed Forces. I am so proud of you and so is your mother.'

I felt emotional and a little more nervous than I already was.

'I have always been a *padaaku* (bookworm), but the Army insists on physical fitness and discipline. I hope I can do it. I hope I don't let you down, *Bauji*'.

He hugged me hard as he said, 'You can never let us down. Our love and blessings are always with you. It's time to heed the call of the nation.'

I bent down to touch his feet. *Jeende Raho!* (May you live long)

His blessings still resound in my ears.

Ab Saunp Diya
Is Jeevan Ka
Bhar Tumhaare Haathon Main
Hai Jeet Tumhare Haathon Main
Aur Haar Tumhaare Haathon Main

I have placed the weight of this life in your hands,
The victory in your hands,
And even my defeat, in your hands.

Krishna Bhajan

1978
Bauji

It was just the two of us who occupied the first-class coupe of the Jammu Tawi Express that seemed to be hurtling towards New Delhi. In a dramatic role reversal, it was I who cradled *Bauji* protectively on my lap while offering him the tiniest of morsels of the simple home-cooked meal packed by my wife, Urmil.

'*Kaka*, I am not able to eat…' he muttered helplessly. I persevered; he could only swallow if he could keep sipping water to keep it down. It was a grim reminder of all the reasons for this sudden train journey to Delhi. I couldn't help but feel a pang of regret.

How could this happen to me? And at a time when I finally had some family time to enjoy? Why did destiny throw a curveball at the exact moment that my life began to look up? There were no answers, just a series of questions. I could only surmise that love and loss follow us everywhere. There was really nothing we were doing wrong when we wished the best for our family, but what felt grossly unfair was just life itself. It did seem to me that good times were about to elude me once again.

'Raja, don't think so much; your frown lines will turn permanent!'

Who said that? I was shaken out of my reverie and in a continuation of this daydream, the soft voice that I heard established the presence of my mother. She may be in another world, but she could read my mind. This vision was just what I needed to come out of my low mood and get rid of the self-reproach that was so much a part of my personality and continued to besiege me even later in life. I pulled myself together and repeated softly to myself, 'I must stay calm and logical.'

And then, I began recalling the chain of events that culminated last Wednesday - the day we light-heartedly called 'meat day.' *Bauji w*as a foodie and a stickler for his favourite meats. He would insist on eating mutton at least one day of the week, and he was willing to do the groundwork needed to make it happen. He was equally thoughtful and sensitive to my pure vegetarian wife. So, he not only purchased but also washed and cleaned the mutton every Wednesday and then assisted her in making his favourite non-vegetarian curry with the addition of a single potato. After years of enjoying this weekly ritual, we all knew something was amiss when he was unable to swallow his favourite food.

The investigations began immediately and we were advised to monitor the symptoms. What began as fatigue and sore throat escalated to hoarseness and weight loss. It was when we met the specialist at the Army Hospital in Jammu Cantonment that our worst fears were confirmed. Our beloved *Bauji* was battling terminal throat cancer that had spread with such little warning.

My thoughts were in a mess. It was hard for me to accept that the most towering personality of my life was at his most fragile. My throat felt parched and I glugged water to ease that dryness, but to no avail. He didn't deserve this illness. He had always been a fit sportsperson whose slim frame belied his age. His disciplined lifestyle, focus on a nutritious diet and his love for fresh air and good company were what kept him energized and inspired us. He was also a devout Brahmin, sans the rigidity, an Urdu and Persian scholar who wrote regularly and artistically in his diary even though he was a master of the Queen's English. Getting up at the crack of dawn, walking for hours, swimming great lengths in summer, never drinking or smoking…he was an example for all of us. This sense of balance and calm was particularly remarkable because he lived through the toil and turmoil of the partition while being employed by the British government without compromising on his principles or his dignity.

More importantly, he was as much family to me as were my wife and three daughters. It was not always like that. There was a time in my life when I dreaded him, avoided him, and even blamed him for my mother's early demise. But that was all way before I really understood him.

As was common in those days, my father was a distant figure in early childhood. For as long as she was around, I could only confide in my mother. It was only after she left me that I began to acknowledge the role played by my father and slowly understand his challenges. It did not take me long to marvel at how beautifully he managed the household and kept our family together, refusing every proposal to remarry even though he was widowed at a rather young age. Our finest bonds were built once he chose to make a home with me, despite the fact that I was the youngest of his three sons and five daughters.

I could not hold back my tears at the realization that the only parent I had known since I was twelve was slipping away. I was helpless to stop the inevitable and could only derive strength and solace by leaning on the faith with which I had grown up.

'When things get tough, surrender to the Almighty,' these eternal words of my mother echoed in my ears as I fought off the drowning feeling. Thinking of her helped me channel my anxiety and my childhood memories instinctively took over. I began humming the song that had been a favourite of my parents. As I began humming his favourite *Bhajan,* which translates as, 'I have placed the weight of this life in your hands, the victory in your hands, And even my defeat, in your hands', I could see *Bauji's* lips move to the lyrics. I sang it louder even though emotions threatened to overwhelm my efforts. The words sounded surreal against the backdrop of the steady chug of the rail engine.

Anticipatory grief washed over me like a giant wave. *Bauji* was not just a devoted father and dependable friend to me but also to my wife, who could count on him during those times when she couldn't count on me. It was no mean feat for my wife and father to hold the fort at a time when uncertainty surrounded them. Sirens and blackouts were the rules when war broke out in 1961, 1965, and 1971 or when I occupied forward posts in remote, far-flung, non-family stations. It was at these times that my father took on the mantle of being the man of the house.

Reminiscences found a way of creeping in as I grappled with memories. Barely 20 years of age, I was introduced to life in the Infantry arm of the Armed Forces, followed by finding a life partner at 24, which gave me much-needed relief from the stresses and strains of an active operational life. And even though I was completely committed to my profession, I was unprepared at how it affected my young wife. It was quite a challenge for her to enjoy marital bliss when my work schedules were this erratic and my combat and operational readiness exercises kept me away from my wife for months at a stretch. It didn't make it easier as she was almost six years my junior and this made it harder for her and for me. I was very conscious that I was an absent son, husband and later a father. At all these moments, it was reassuring to know that my own father's support to my wife and three daughters was unflappable.

I allowed myself a little smile as I remembered one of my daughters asking how the creators of the dining table with six chairs knew that *Bauji* lived with us. We would encourage the girls to share these observations with their grandad, who would clap with glee or laugh delightedly at their innocence.

Ah! What a vibrant and cheerful home it was…one where every birthday celebration was charming because my father loved to sing the birthday song in his own version. 'Happy, happy, happy', he would join with childlike excitement while the children enjoyed his infectious energy.

This is how he managed to achieve something few parents can do so effortlessly – integrating himself seamlessly into the very fabric of his children's and grandchildren's lives in such a wonderful way that none of us could even imagine life without him.

My father was a change agent in his own unique way. A staunch advocate of equality and empowerment, he raised his own daughters - my sisters - with the best of education and opportunities. Remarkably enough, even in the 1940s, my sisters were qualified working women, highly sought after and respected by their respective grooms. It was this pride in parenting girls that was part of our family ethos. He was equally vocal in telling off anyone who expressed sympathies or remonstrated with my wife about birthing three girls.

As a matter of fact, he had even taken the liberty to chastise my wife's *dadi* when she expressed her sympathies at the birth of the third girl and remonstrated, 'Poor Urmil, this young girl has three daughters. What a difficult burden to carry. My prayers are with her and the girls...'

It so happened that *Bauji* heard this remark and exploded, making my wife's grandma flee the place, saying, '*Tauba Tauba…*' (God help me)

'*Teen Deviyan (*three Goddesses) have blessed our home. Who asked you to pray for us or even sympathise with us? If you have nothing better to say to us, you should leave right now. You are not welcome in this home anymore.'

Behind this rude reprimand was a loving heart. Even the chastised lady could not hold it against him because his pride in his daughter-in-law and granddaughters came from such a good place. It's a different matter that she never dared set foot in our house in his presence despite our reassurances.

My wife was truly touched by this progressiveness. This thoughtful show of solidarity, especially at a time when she was being given the most pitiful looks for bearing girls, was very special to her. It may even have been a factor that contributed to her lifelong devotion to him even though he was a disciplinarian in his own way who insisted on strict timings for his meals.

I often wondered how she could manage to be a dutiful daughter-in-law as well as a friend and confidant to him and defend him spiritedly, even in front of her own father and siblings who would see her serving him selflessly. Never one to shy away from sharing an honest opinion, she would openly appreciate his commitment to our family while recognising her father-in-law as a sensitive man and an affectionate grandfather.

Bauji stirred restlessly and all my fears came rushing back. I would have never agreed for him to travel at a time when he was seriously unwell, but I could not disregard the requests of my siblings, who wanted an opportunity to be closer to him in his final days. My wife and I discussed it the previous night and agreed that not only would we have an opportunity to get the best medical facilities in a place like Delhi, but it would also cheer him up to meet everyone. Since time was running out, the doctors felt it would not be advisable to delay travel. It was under these compelling circumstances that I booked tickets for both of us almost instantly.

The toughest part was convincing him. My wife and I tried to cheer him up as we reminded him that he would be meeting all his daughters and sons, but he was unresponsive and adamant. The illness seemed to have sucked the enthusiasm out of him.

'Don't pack so many clothes, Urmil. I plan to come back home very soon,' he looked at her pleadingly.

She attempted to smile while she placated him.

'No harm in taking a little extra *Bauji*...so many people will visit you and you must dress well. I promise I will join you once the girls have their vacations.'

He turned his attention back to me.

'You are both looking after me, Prithvi...why do we even need to leave? Promise me, *Kaka,* you will bring me back soon. My *Siya Ram* await- my arrival back at the temple here.' My frail father mumbled.

On the day of the journey, he was aloof and distant, disinterested in seeing anyone except his beloved Gods in his temple at R S Pura in Jammu Cantonment. Tears blurred my vision as my father drifted in and out of sleep, sighing and groaning periodically. The choked feeling returns as my mind is plagued with myriad inane questions.

'Who would oversee the grades of the girls? Who would chat with their school principal and oversee their progress? Would my wife be able to handle all the responsibilities of home in my absence? And what about the people he loved socialising with? How would they react when I returned without him? He was such an integral part of the house parties where my seniors, my colleagues and even the junior officers loved the way he counselled them. And then, for no reason, another strange thought bothered me. How would we ever relish Meat Wednesdays again?'

This cycle of self-pity, which was creeping onto me repeatedly, was unfair to my father. While I could see that, I could not stop feeling sorry for myself. It was a herculean effort to remind myself not to be self-centred and that I needed to focus on *Bauji*. He was the one who was ill and all I needed to do was to care for him and support him through this final phase of life.

'Tell me my favourite story, *Bauji*?' I whispered into his ear.

While the pain medications were a necessity, I was relieved that he continued to be mentally agile and lucid even through this tough journey. He responded with disarming innocence, narrating the story of my birth in a soft yet clear voice.

'You were born on December 9, 1936 at 42, Fauj Square, behind Gole Market, Delhi. We lived in a big government quarter allotted to me as I worked at the Viceroy's office at that time. I came back home early on 8th December as your mother went into labour in the afternoon and I prayed all day waiting for the news. All I wanted was a healthy baby and the good health of my dear Prem. We had the best midwife, and I made sure she had the best facilities. I remember how restless I was as I heard her moaning in pain all night. The stars and moon gave way to a glow that spread across the skies.

Chidyaa, the midwife, burst out of the room.

'Kaka Aaya' (a boy has arrived), shouted the middle-aged *daima* (midwife) and the home filled with joy.

His eyes twinkled with recollection.

'I immediately gifted her a gold necklace that my wife had reserved for the long-expected event. Our family priest made your horoscope, giving you the secret name Pradyumn. This is the name of Krishna and Rukmini's son. The name I announced to the world was Prithvi. You were born Pandit Prithvi Nath Kumaria. I told your mother that you would be the pride and joy of our family. She called you 'Raja,' the enlightened prince.'

He seemed to have gotten a fresh surge of energy through these recollections, but now he was drained from the effort. As I adjusted his pillow to make him comfortable, I caught a glance at the picture he always carried in his wallet.

A black and white family portrait of my stylish father in riding breeches, long boots and a hard hat standing next to my beautiful mother draped in a simple cream-coloured saree with the *pallu* covering her head while she was surrounded by all 8 of us reminded me of the image of Ram and Sita in our home. Set against the majestic backdrop of Shimla's Mall Road with snow-clad trees visible behind us, made this one of the most soothing images of my short-lived childhood, a reminder of the joys of large families.

Being the seventh of a total of eight children was an experience that I cherish. As my eyes locked onto the eyes of the curly-haired little person in a well-ironed shirt and shorts, a miniature me reflected a zest for life, which I struggled to recall in this difficult time.

It was just the reminder that I sorely needed and as I looked at my ailing father, I could only salute the man who kept it all together and gave us a comfortable home, the best of education and facilities that only the elite or the British could afford. We had an enviable childhood, the most idyllic vacations, with cherished horse-riding lessons. And then we moved to Shimla, the summer Capital of the British and to Glendale in Himachal Pradesh in a luxury typically reserved for Indian royalty. I was a handful, courting trouble and putting my nose into matters that did not concern me. It could have been the special treatment meted out to me that made me feel like a little prince. Being protected and nurtured can do wonders for one's self-confidence and I was a bundle of energy and enthusiasm in those golden days when my father's protection and security and my mother's beautiful umbrella of love and concern kept my spirits high.

My father is mumbling in his sleep, but it sounds like a pleasant dream as he calls out the name that epitomises love, evoking the fondest memories of my childhood.

'Prem.... Prem....*tu kithhe hain* (where are you)?' he repeats her name in his sleep a few times, looking for her, searching for her presence as he continues to mutter.

'Your mother is so proud...so happy...look at her smile.'

I felt the tears slide down noiselessly, not willing to wipe them away, allowing them to wash my face. I felt cleansed, ready to meet the rest of the family that were waiting at the station to receive their father.

Vaishnav Jan

Ko Tene Kahiye Jay

Peer Parayee

Jaane Ray

A true devotee of the Lord is one
Who feels the pain of others
And works to relieve their suffering.

Gandhiji's favourite *Bhajan* by Narsi Mehta

1948
Prem

Prem. A name that spelt love and embodied purity and compassion, affection and togetherness. In one of her rare photos, as I see her hazel eyes smile back at me, it is as if I can see my soul reflected in hers because we both have the same light eyes. The legacy lives on as I see them continue in my progeny.

A bustling family like ours was not uncommon in those days. While the senior male member of the house was inevitably busy, aloof or absent, the women overcompensated by being expressive and overly affectionate towards the children even when they were immersed in cooking for a large tribe of children with age gaps that could extend from two to twenty. In such an atmosphere, the youngsters of the family created their own pastime with hardly any parental influence or interference.

I was an exception. The youngest son of a large family, I never strayed too far from my mother. And her area of influence was dominated by the large kitchen, where I would love to sit with her. I had her blessings to make it my very own play area while getting familiar with all those fascinating kitchen implements, just as long as I didn't come too close to the hot *Chulah (*stove*)*. This was my territory and it was far more attractive than the company of my siblings or my toys. I flourished amidst those traditional utensils like the *Karahi's*, the *Parats,* the *Chakla Belan and* the *Chimta* just so that I would continue to be the favourite of my mother. Her planning and organisational skills were admirable and best of all, she never needed to raise her voice. Her self-belief and quiet confidence made her a natural leader, but it was her compassion and humility that made me wary of ever hurting her and won the hearts of the helpers who she supervised so effortlessly.

I felt important when I was seated next to her, proud to be a part of the process that resulted in the most mouth-watering food. The heady aroma of *desi ghee* on a hot *aloo parantha* or the sizzling *hing jeera tarkaa* (seasonings) on my favourite *peeli daal* (yellow lentil curry) is a dear memory of those blissful days. On special days, the men prepared mutton curry, but it was the ladies who did the prepping and the cleaning and I was always a member of the ladies' clan. I had an ulterior motive, as I wanted to ensure my mother had kept aside enough of at least some of these delicious dishes to feed herself. As an impressionable young boy, I had already picked up on the casualness with which matters like women's health and nutrition were ignored.

This could be disastrous for those like my mother, who always put their families before them. So, as family members gathered for the meals that were being served by the women, I recall insisting that I would like to eat later with my mother. This was considered stubbornness by some of my family members but I was focused only on her wellbeing and knew that the only way I could convince her to keep some of the best food stuff aside. She was touched by my gesture and I, who was utterly devoted to her, was basking in the glow of her love and pride.

Another place I loved to frequent was my parent's bedroom. This was a sacred, secluded retreat, cut off from the rest of the house to ensure that my father was not disturbed by the chatter and clutter that the rest of the family lived in. No one dared to be seen here without his explicit permission. No one except me. And I was as discreet as possible, though there was no way I could have escaped my father's eagle eyes. Clearly, he allowed this liberty only for the love of his life, my mother, his dearest wife.

This room was the closest I could get to heaven. To begin with, it smelt of my mother's favourite talcum powder, interspersed with *ittar* (perfume). Sometimes, I quietly peeped into my father's cupboard and was overwhelmed by his collection of shirts and ties and well-polished shoes, just like the English *Sahibs*. If I entered just after my father left, I would be assailed by my father's English scent, one that smelt a lot like shoe polish. As far as possible, I avoided visiting if my father's scent lingered. Many years later, I would miss this very fragrance, but at the time, it was my mother who dominated my affections.

While I admired the way my sisters and their friends wore colourful and fashionable clothes, I loved the fact that my mother favoured simplicity. She was partial to neutral colours and to cotton *sarees*. It was only during the time spent in Shimla that we would see a different version of her as she draped a thick coat or shawl over her saree. Her head was always covered, and she smelled beautiful. It was later that I learnt that this was her only indulgence – this love for fragrances. I enjoyed watching her hum a *bhajan* (prayer) as she got ready every morning, rubbing loose talcum powder on her face, placing a red *bindi* (vermilion dot) on her forehead and covering her head with the *pallu* (border) of her sari. This simple yet classic look defined beauty in every way.

Everyone in our house acknowledged my special bond with my mother. But this acknowledgement cost me heavily as I was made to feel guilty for this bonding. Ever since I can remember, I was teased mercilessly for my refusal to wean away from my mother's breast milk even after I began school.

My father was particularly strict and would reprimand me sharply if he caught me. My mother would give him a pacifying look and argue with him that it was harmless. He would sometimes let it go or laugh it off, but at other times, his irritability was apparent. Mother hated having to justify this special attachment to me and my youngest sister, Rani. I often wonder if she continued this physical bonding with her two youngest children because she had a premonition that we would both get the least amount of time with her. Is that why she gave all of herself in the limited time she had with us? Whatever may be the reason, we knew she loved us wholeheartedly and that our world was complete because of her. I particularly felt blessed by her unstinted love.

Even though her support for us was unconditional, she was equally mindful of teaching us the right values. Stories from the scriptures were a part of our upbringing and her constant reminder that I was born with a bigger purpose and must be worthy and deserving of it helped me stay grounded. Even when I was being naughty and mischievous, she would lovingly explain to me the consequences of my actions without being judgemental.

One incident that I remember rather clearly was when we lived at Lodhi Road in Delhi, just after the riots broke out in 1947. As rioting mobs went on a rampage against a specific community, a curfew was imposed and within minutes, the streets were secluded. Amidst the sirens and the police vigilance, the *Tonga* driver named Abdul, who often moved on the streets outside our home, was forced to flee with his family.

As I peeped out of the window, he placed his finger on his lips to gesture to me not to call out as he tied his horse outside our home. I took it as a sign that he trusted me to take care of his precious animal. My family protested at my excitement to feed the horse and pet it as if it were my own, but I took my duties rather seriously and began befriending the agitated horse. Honoured to be given this responsibility, I succumbed to my childish excitement and impulsively decided to mount my horse the very next day. Needless to say, the horse, clearly upset with the loss of his master, reared its head and brought me down to earth. I got a rude reality check as I fell to the ground. Even though I was badly hurt, it was my pride that took the beating. As my friends and neighbours laughed at my plight, some of them remonstrating about my habit of inviting trouble, I glanced at my mother, who looked concerned at my injuries. She not only nursed me to health but also patiently and kindly guided me to understand the importance of the event that had just transpired.

'*Kaka*, you were meant to be the caretaker of the horse, not its owner. People who have been displaced due to the partition need your support, but this must be selfless. Focus on helping them, but do not try to assert your power over something that doesn't belong to you. It is not correct for you to claim Abdul's property as your own. And that is why this horse would not accept you. It pines for its owner, so you must let it go. Allow the authorities to send him back to Abdul or to someone who can care for it.'

While I longed to ride Abdul's horse, I felt compassion for the horse and as I listened to her carefully, I realised that her words made sense. More than anything, I deeply respected a point of view that was logical and kind at the same time. The horse was eventually sent to the lost and found department as we were unable to locate the owner and I was left sadder but wiser after this episode. As I look back, I am glad I heeded her wise counsel.

Another time, Tejinder, a Sikh refugee from Lahore, shouting *'Chhole, Chhole'* got me activated. When asked why he had to move around in the heat, he revealed that he was selling boiled chickpeas as he had no other means of earning a livelihood ever since they had to leave their belongings and start afresh. I was taken aback to see the suffering of a boy who seemed to be so close to my age but was toiling so hard that he had turned all sweaty and tired. I could think of no other way to help him except by lightening his load. In my excitement to be helpful, I not only offered to carry his *Matki* (pot) on my head and help him sell his wares but also begged my friends to buy his food. He protested, but I was adamant. I was not prepared for what followed. I was mercilessly mocked for befriending someone of a far lower status and my own siblings complained to my father that I was always up to some new activity that would cause trouble. These were the times when my mother's warm hug and loving advice about following one's heart, even if it meant being oblivious to the opinions of others, did wonders for my self-confidence.

The horrors of the partition were unending and even as a young boy, I was very alert to the polarised environment around us. It was important not to be a silent spectator at a time when there was so much emotion and angst. My school teachers also encouraged us to be agents of social change and I was personally conscious of the need for peace during such violent times. At the same time, I could not help but support those freedom fighters who laid down their lives for the nation. And that is why I felt somewhat redeemed when we studied Bharatendu Harishchandra's famous literary work *Vaidik Hinsa Na Hinsa Bhavti,* (violence is justified if the cause is right) in school. I was moved. It prompted me to activate a group of boys and girls to be a part of a drama club. In the very first meeting, we decided that we would invite people for an amateur street theatre activity that would propagate the theme of nonviolence.

But when we went door to door, inviting the neighbours to see the play, we met with a lot of rejections and mocking. Imagine my delight when I received the wholehearted support of my mother. I was doubly thrilled when I spotted my mother sitting amongst the audience with her *satsang* friends just to cheer us on. Her validation and appreciation gave me the confidence to pursue my love for drama while also continuing on a lifelong journey of being a warrior, a peaceful ally, as much as an agent of social change.

There were many such touching moments in the limited time that I had with my mother. When I volunteered to buy vegetables and fruits from the market, I was obsessed with impressing her. The only way I could make her see me as an astute and sensible shopper was to pretend that I could bargain, and I would misquote how much I paid for the vegetables and fruits and use my own pocket money to cover the difference. When she discovered what I had been doing, instead of scolding me, she simply hugged me and cried, 'Oh *Raja*, you do not need to impress me or anyone'

I would like to count on all these distant memories to keep her alive in my heart, but I am often assailed by other memories. Much as I try to brush them away, I close my eyes and see the garlanded photo of my beloved mother in the middle of the courtyard as I return from school.

Our happy and peaceful home was a jarring cacophony of sounds that ranged from loud wailing and chest beating to garish displays of grief. As was the custom in those days, groups of professional female mourners trooped into our house. They proceeded to call out her name in high-pitched screams while interspersing it with the wailing sounds *'hai... hai'* as they violently beat their breasts.

It was the thundering voice of my grief-stricken father that finally broke through the pandemonium.

'Stop this, *Siyaappa*...(mourning) leave us in peace...go away, all of you.'

The shocked gathering fell silent. His face was red with fury, even as his eyes looked swollen after crying all night. It was as if his grief had found an outlet in anger, which was in full flow now. The mourners recovered from their shock and slowly began to walk out in a single file down the long hallway, which was laid out with pristine white sheets. Her framed image, like an enigmatic Mona Lisa, with her slight smile, watched the bizarre proceedings benignly.

Even a twelve-year-old like myself realised that this outburst was a result of months of stress and tension ever since my mother took ill. There was a reason why my father erupted when he saw the mourners. It came from the remnants of anguish that he had kept tightly bottled up ever since my mother insisted on attending the post-funeral ceremonies of her brother even when she was seriously ill with high blood pressure and breathing difficulties. Her health declined quite rapidly and dramatically from the time that she joined the mourning party. It was later discovered that my mother had fainted while attempting to join this obnoxious custom that many reformers had also tried to erase.

When we lost her to a cardiac arrest, it was as if our worst nightmares were coming true. My father held the mourners and their regressive customs responsible for her death. As a young boy, I was heartbroken when my older siblings whispered that her heart was weak. I remember even wondering how someone as large-hearted as my mother could be termed weak of heart.

After her brother's sad demise, she was confined to her bed for weeks. But even during those difficult days, her love for her family and nation was active and unwavering. She has been the woman who continued to support India's freedom struggle even while her husband worked at the Viceroy's office and was thrilled at the announcement of independence.

'*Bapuji* has been shot!'

I can still hear this shocking announcement as a young boy ran up and down the road, screaming himself hoarse.

She, who had shed tears for every freedom fighter who chose to sacrifice and became *'Shaheed'* was heartbroken to hear of Gandhiji's martyrdom.

My young, impressionable heart skipped a beat. This was the worst kind of news at a time when the country was limping back to normalcy. Our family was plunged into grief. My mother was inconsolable. The Mahatma was her God, her redeemer; the man who we all called 'Father of the Nation' was gone. It was a huge blow to my mother, who was ailing at the time. She called out to my brother Surinder.

'*Kuku,* go quickly to the exact spot where *Bapuji* died. Bring some *mitti* (earth) from the spot below *Bapu's* head. I want to keep it in my temple in this silver cup.' She implored.

'I also want to go with him…can I go, please?' I begged, not wanting to be left out for such an important assignment.

'Yes, *Kaka*, you can go too. But hold on tight to your brother,' she patted my cheek and then addressed my brother.

'Take *Kaka* also, but be very careful. I hear there is a big crowd there. Keep an eye on your little brother…don't let go of his hand.'

We barely understood the importance of what we were asked to do, but those tender words continued to evoke sweet memories, making me forget my sadness. I perch myself on the handlebar of Surinder's cycle and he begins pedalling furiously to the hallowed spot, all the way from Sir Harcourt Butler School, near Birla Mandir, to the spot which is now Rajghat.

We must have had a size advantage because we managed to sneak in and sneak out holding fistfuls of precious earth just minutes before a full-blown stampede was reported as the distraught public rushed to catch a last glimpse of their favourite leader. This was a poignant moment so soon after the partition, which had already affected the collective psyche of the nation. Gandhiji lived and died for the country and my mother's deep connection to the true freedom fighters of this nation ensured that I and my brother recorded this momentous event for posterity with this simple act.

That day will also go down in history as possibly the last time we spoke to my mother in such detail. Just two months after Gandhiji's martyrdom, my mother was seriously ill and was rushed to the nearby Government hospital late in the night. I woke up to a melee and a missing mother.

No one would tell me where she was. Not even that she would never ever come home. And when they finally did, I refused to accept it.

It was far too painful and even today, I prefer to block this memory. All I recall is running frantically towards that very same hospital where I banged my little hands against their gates, but they wouldn't let a teary eyed young boy come in without an adult.

I walked back home and cried for days. What was life without a mother? I saw no reason to carry on. It was the sadness in my youngest sister Rani's eyes that finally made me realise that my mother's untimely demise was heartbreaking for everyone but more so for my little sister, who would look at me and the siblings for support.

I was too young to understand the importance of this event and for a brief moment, I blamed my father for not taking care of her. I even blamed God for letting this happen. And I definitely blamed the doctors for failing in their duty to cure her.

I even blamed myself. ' I did not give her the attention and love she deserved,' I berated myself, all the while wondering if there was anything we could have done to save her.

The loss of my mother became such a low point of my young life that it even made me drift away from my widowed father, who was equally consumed with grief and immersed himself with renewed vigour in his work. It was only a few weeks later that I noticed the toll it was taking on my father, who seemed to wither away.

'It must have been the stress and the careless habits of eating leftovers,' my distraught father voiced my concerns as he grieved her.

A young widower, my father refused all matrimonial alliances that came his way and chose to remain single till his death – a testimony to his love and commitment to his family and to his late wife.

Years later, my father still could not shake off the grief and continued to miss and love my mother to the exclusion of everything else.

My sisters rallied around, mothering me and my youngest sister, Rani, while keeping an eye on my father's well-being. It was no easy task to handle a pampered, insecure and confused boy like myself. Under the garb of intellectualism, I hid my fears about love and loss and the uncertainty of the future.

These circumstances resulted in a most difficult and rebellious adolescence and I found myself being moved from my brother's home to my sister's home and back to father far too often. This constant movement was frustrating and I longed for some stability.

I was barely 12 when I made the decision to move to Rohtak, where my eldest sister Kaushalya, almost 15 years my senior, lived with her husband. My *Jijajee,* a venerable professor at Rohtak University who was popularly acknowledged as *Shastriji,* was an inspiration for me and became my true mentor till the very end.

My sister had all the qualities of my mother and living with her was the closest I could get to the same pure love and affection. Along with love and peace, their home also gave me the intellectual enlightenment and wisdom that was much needed to cope with the challenges I faced since my mother passed away. It was in this household that I blended so well and I felt heard and understood. So complete was my assimilation that everyone in Rohtak believed I was the second son to my *Jijajee,* Professor Prabhu Datt Shastri, M.A, MOL.

It was a brand-new start at the Rohtak Vaish School, where I jumped from Class 7 to Class 9. Additionally I got an opportunity to become Captain of the cricket team. A few weeks into the system, and I was also a member of the Drama Club. All went well for a while till my charmed existence ended abruptly.

My confidence and charisma got me into the good books of teachers, but I was no match for a bunch of school bullies who threatened my nephew, Manmohan, better known as *Buku. Buku* was not just a dearest friend and brother but a maths genius to boot. I was not willing to see him being bullied, so in my enthusiasm to assist him, I put my foot in my mouth by threatening them that my brother *Kuku* would come from Delhi and deal with each one of them. And this is how I built my gentle brother as a great bully himself, pretending that he was a gang leader of sorts by calling him the *Dada* of Delhi.

Once the threat was blurted out, I panicked. Surinder was the non-violent type and would never agree to be a part of this or even approve of such exaggeration. I dared not call him.

But there is a God and miracle of miracles, he was on my side. I returned from school that day to see my dearest brother Surinder waiting for me at my sister's home.

Assuming he had come to make good my hollow claim and take up the challenge of beating up the bullies, I urged him to come with me to meet the bullies. He flatly refused, much to my disappointment. He then revealed his real purpose for coming as a visit to take me back home from Rohtak.

'*Bauji* misses you…I, too, cannot live in Delhi without you next to me. It is high time, Prithvi, let's go back,' he said in his characteristically straightforward and loving manner.

Perhaps those bullies lurking in the background had overwhelmed me, or maybe it was the genuineness of Surinder's appeal; I just couldn't say no. He was not just my brother but a part of me, my true soulmate. Truth be told, I missed him too. We applied for a migration certificate back to Sir Harcourt Butler School in Delhi the same day and within a week, we returned home after a teary goodbye to Rohtak.

Despite this move back to Delhi, my eldest sister and *Jijajee* (brother in law) continued to play a major part in my life, even after my marriage, as my wife Urmil moved to Hissar for the completion of her B.A and my niece Shashi became so close to my wife that she lived with us at Beas some years later.

Back in Delhi, I recall becoming a bit of a leader myself. It must have been this love for public speaking and elocution that resulted in my playing a huge part in the school Parliament as 'Leader of Opposition'. On one occasion, I even got a chance to play Lord Ram during the annual *Ram Leela* (Tableau depicting the life of Lord Rama). I also enjoyed helping students revise and brush up before exams. Principal S. Lal of Harcourt Butler School, who was also a mentor to me, had also played his part in encouraging me to return to Delhi. In the midst of this hectic schedule of studies and co-curricular activities, once I was back in Delhi, I came in touch with Sardar Hukum Singh, an NRI settled in the USA, who convinced me of the dire requirement for an organisation where young boys and girls could interact with each other through confidential Post Box Numbers. He called it SOS, giving it a kind of legitimacy and recruited a few boys, including me. I was his star worker, and he identified me by the enthusiasm and passion that I displayed at one of the events at my school. He called me to his office opposite the Regal Cinema. I was thrilled to be handpicked and happy to be employed while in school. The work was simple. Each member who subscribed to this service was allotted a separate post box with its own key to collect mail and interact. There was also a provision for them to meet in a hall, which they could book over the weekend to get to know each other. This must have been a prelude to the dating apps that are so popular today, but at the time, I had no idea what it meant and who I was colluding with. Of course, the supreme confidentiality of this exercise was a giveaway given the conservative societal norms of those times, but to me, this highly secretive operation gave an unprecedented thrill, and of course, there was the monetary reward coupled with the satisfaction of bringing young people together. And for all of this, I was paid a princely salary of ₹ 10 with a bonus if I could coordinate the evening activity every week.

This operation carried on for many months. Rather, as long as the pocket money fuelled my hunger for books, which I could now borrow or buy without guilt. Looking back, it also seems possible that I introduced the book club concept by creating a membership base and challenging them to complete a book. Sometimes, if we were lucky, we even saw the adaptation at Regal Cinema.

These were my cherished outings with my pals with juicy mangoes for company. As and when we could afford it, we would finish off our movie outings with a round of *Chole Bhature.*

These part-time jobs gave me plenty of confidence and a degree of financial freedom, but they also took away precious time, which I wanted to channel into my love for reading and dramatics. My academics were also suffering from a lack of time. To make matters worse, some family members decided that I was undisciplined and needed supervision.

'Where do you think these books are going to take you? Sitting around and reading all day will only make you fat or lazy or both.'

This below-the-belt remark was made by one of my close relatives and on one occasion, it hit home harder than ever. It also became a wake-up call for me. Always academically inclined, I was accustomed to being mocked by family members as a *padaaku* whose head was in the clouds. But I had never nurtured any self-doubt until that time. These remarks were unpleasant, but they were equally worrisome. Would I never be able to make anything of myself? I was forced to do some self-reflection, and in that sense, this taunt helped me focus.

I suddenly had a goal – something to prove to those who imagined I was incapable of anything else. It was exactly the sort of challenge a restless teenager needed to achieve their objective. Not many believed that I could get through UPSC. Principal Lal even challenged me. 'Go ahead, try; I guarantee you won't be able to pass.'

A bookworm with a passion for creative arts, I was an unlikely candidate for the Indian Army in the 1950s. All hell broke loose as word got out that I was preparing to join the Indian Army. In those days, we were expected to clear a fairly tough UPSC exam, so their cynicism was justified. Little did these people know that I was not just any teenager but one who was driven to fulfil their destiny. And my commitment and perseverance paid off. Not only did I manage a fabulous 74.6 percent as my UPSC score and a rather respectable 75 percent at Sir Harcourt Butler Higher Secondary School, New Delhi, in Class 11, but I also aced the detailed Service Selection Board (SSB) interview, which is a psychological assessment of prospective officers. The intensive medicals that followed this process were equally challenging, but once all these hurdles were cleared, I was eligible for the elite Indian Armed Forces.

My heart surged with pride at this selection, even though I was nervous about the tough training that I would undergo. I felt a step closer to my life's purpose and was excited to step into a role that I seemed to have been born for. My mother's warrior ancestry and my father's scholar–soldier lineage meant that I was preparing myself to serve the nation. I had my mother's blessings and my father's wholehearted support. I felt ready to take on the challenge.

Two stars on the shoulder are worth more than billions in the sky.

1954
Dehradun

The steam engine that was chugging from Delhi seemed to be huffing and puffing up the steep slope from Haridwar to Dehradun. Finally, the train stopped with a long sigh. We had arrived.

I disembarked from the train lugging a steel trunk and a bedding cum holdall which had all my possessions rolled into them. Gawking with fascination at my surroundings, I was just another awkward teenager – all of 15 years who had boarded the train leaving Delhi Railway station late last night and somehow transformed by the time we arrived at the destination the very next day.

Sharp whistles silenced the commotion that fluttered all around. Amidst the cacophony of orders, one voice stood out.

'Future Cadets, bring your luggage out and stand in front of your compartment.'

We stood at attention in three rows and were now facing an imposing 6 feet 3 inches tall, red-faced Major R.S. Ayling. Irish Cold Stream Grenadier Guards Regimental Sergeant Ayling was a gentleman on deputation from the British Army and came with impressive credentials. He would be the designated person who would be responsible for training us and instilling officer-like qualities whether we joined the Army, the Navy or the Air Force. It was his job to transform the raw, sometimes unruly teenage boys into gentlemen cadets of the three services in their respective academies. This was certainly no mean task and one he mastered even when the words of command changed to Hindi.

'Gentlemen, pay attention'

His authoritative voice boomed at us. There was pin-drop silence as he began to address us in his distinctive and rather exceptional style.

'Listen to me very carefully because I never repeat myself. Your 'mummy' and 'daddy' are not here, nor are they expected to be. From this moment on, the Army is your father and your mother. If you follow orders and respect this institution, we are here to take care of you. Is that clear?'

His voice rose to a crescendo when he asked the rhetorical question. We did what was expected of us and roared in unison.

'Yes, Sir!'

'Now pick up all your luggage and start following the guides who will help you move to your respective Squadrons. I am watching every step or misstep along the way, so better not lag or slack off!'

We were suitably impressed but equally wary of what was in store for us as the great movement began. Our luggage and bedding were carried in the 3 Tonners to arrive at the erstwhile Italian Prisoners of War Barracks of Clement Town. The transition was overwhelming and exhilarating at the same time. A brand-new location that would give a brand-new start to my life.

My first day in the Baker Squadron of the Indian Army at the Joint Services Wing Clement Town was certainly not a bed of roses. After a tough day of academics followed by drills, riding, and swimming, we rushed to the boiler room for a hot water bath, only to find ourselves at the far end of the long queues. It was here that we were introduced to a group of seniors who were just waiting to rag us. Perhaps ragging is not the best word because it bore no resemblance to the sort of ragging one hears about in academic institutes. Our seniors took it upon themselves to familiarise us with the nitty-gritty of the academy and prepare us rookies for the challenges ahead of us. This was more of an unofficial induction into the trials, tribulations, and vagaries of cadet life.

Being a bit of a nerd, fitness was never my forte, and this is where I faced the harsh reality of physicals, which were so tough that even the fittest guy felt humbled. The more I struggled, the more likely I was to be picked on by the seniors first. This could be attributed to my noticeable chubbiness and my outwardly soft demeanor, or likely due to my subpar running skills, which were exposed on the very first day.

This made me increasingly insecure, more so as I knew that in the NDA, every challenge needed to be faced as there was no place to hide. In that sense, the ragging turned out to be a lucky charm because once the seniors decided to work on me, I became their challenge and they began motivating me to perform better. I was initially goaded into running at odd hours by them to improve my performance, and since this was beyond the official training, it was backbreaking, but I had no choice. As if all of this were not enough, I was subjected to innumerable front rolls, back rolls, cream rolls, sit-ups, crunches and much more.

There were too many moments when I felt defeated and on the verge of breaking down. But I would remind myself that I came from a warrior ancestry and that I had all the qualities in me to be a soldier. This self-talk is what kept me going along with the camaraderie that we were developing amongst us. Academy was home to us and home consisted of spartan cabins that housed up to eight cadets with the barest of necessities and communal bathrooms, which soon became a new way of life, one that was independent yet interdependent.

I often resorted to utilising the visualization techniques that I had practised in drama class in school as I imagined myself leading troops into battle while convincing myself that I was physically and mentally capable of taking on any challenge. I was also strengthening my mind and training myself to remain composed even when circumstances got tough.

At that time, I was too young to understand that I had this precious gift of an ability that was an essential survival technique and that I could use this power of manifesting to my advantage. It was much later that I realised that I was preparing myself to survive not just the tough life of the Armed Forces but the challenges that came even after I retired.

The Armed Forces prides itself on OLQ (Officer Like Qualities) and in keeping with these traditions, even our ragging was 'Officer-like.' Just like Rome, these qualities cannot be expected to be built in a day. The focus on loyalty, camaraderie and dedication to duty was a long process and we were being inducted into the *Fauji* (army men) system bit by bit as carefully planned and stipulated challenges were laid out for us with the specific intent of making us physically and mentally tough. The only way I could convince myself not to run away from this rigour was when I began to appreciate the discipline it brought into my life. That, along with the signs that were liberally strewn inside the academy, constantly reminded us that 'The more we sweat in peace, the less we would bleed in war.'

Ours was an experimental course, with senior termers determined to turn us into soldiers par excellence. Whether the challenges were tough or impossible, there was no mercy shown to us. And there was no chance of complaining. Even if we ever dared to do such a thing, we were reminded of the *mantra, Jitna Ragda Utna Tagda,* which meant that the tougher it got, the fitter we became.

From making our beds neatly to organising and storing our uniforms and clothes and every belonging in cupboards and lockers. This was also the time when many of my batchmates began to pack their bags and run away from this rigour, or *ragda* as it was called. Others could be heard crying through the night. This exodus became far more real when one of my close friends, Bibekananda, an intelligent and upright man who later became a journalist, abruptly left the academy without as much as a goodbye.

That night, I battled self-doubt for the very first time and had a serious self-talk.

'Is this worth it? Wouldn't I rather be a professor or an administrator like my father and uncles?'

I also reflected on what really bothered me the most as I asked myself that eternal question, which always puts maximum pressure on most young people in their teenage years.

'What would my relatives say if I returned?

This wavering was temporary, I reminded myself. Despite the doubts that plagued us newbies, the desire to find a purpose in life and to prove our detractors wrong lit a fire in every belly and strengthened our resolve. The answers came fast and furious and my doubts simply melted away when dawn broke. I trusted my deep-seated instinct that I could not fail in this mission. Before long, I could finally say that my head and heart were in tandem once again. And however tough things were right now, I knew they were bound to pass and so I decided to stick it out.

Today, I look back at these memories with a hint of amusement, but at that time, I was rather traumatised even though I had told myself that quitting was not even an option for me. While this refusal to quit went on to become my strength, it would also take a serious toll on my well-being.

Being plump and unwieldy, I had struggled from the very first day to keep up with the batch. It took me the longest time to get into shape and I must take credit for my willingness to take the toughest route possible. This included hours and hours of long, lonely runs wearing a great coat that ensured a steady stream of sweat running down my body. But I never gave up and after weeks and months of parades and punishments, my efforts bore fruit as I transformed into a swifter, fitter and far suppler version - much better than I could even dream of becoming.

This metamorphosis was not just the result of the tough processes of the Indian Army but also the change that I personally manifested because I knew I wanted to be that warrior who never gave up.

With fitness setting in, I began to prepare myself to ace the other intricacies of Armed Forces life. There was a right way to do everything. The ones that seemed to take most of my time were those innumerable uniforms that needed to be maintained with military perfection. That, along with thirteen nail-studded boots and our paratrooper cycles. It could be something as innocuous as adherence to social etiquette at the dining table in the Cadets' Mess or a surprise inspection of cabins where minor defaults like the folding of a handkerchief could result in *Patti Parades* (changing Uniforms in stipulated time frames) after dinner.

Dinner, in any case, was another parade. God forbid, if you started the soup before the seniors or continued eating once they stopped, there was hell to pay. We were perpetually hungry boys and at the very same time, we had to maintain the highest sense of table manners while eating! This is a conundrum that makes me smile as I look back and feel gratitude for training that made us Officers and Gentlemen of the best types!

Even a minor mistake at the Drill Square would lead to extra drills, extra restrictions and punishments galore. Between the official punishments handed out like candy by Drill Instructors, PT Instructors & Divisional Officers and the unofficial punishments that the seniors gave us, we spent all our waking moment just running, rolling, gasping and moaning or, on the tougher days, lifting our bicycles way above our head and running while someone screams, 'faster, faster.' I learnt what it meant to be exhausted to the point that we could be fast asleep even while standing with our eyes wide open. As frequent inspections became a part of life, we realised that if we did not want any more punishments, we had to align ourselves with a disciplined lifestyle sooner rather than later.

One person who completely oversaw this transition from gawky boys to smartly turned-out young officers was our Adjutant, Captain M. L Wig, well known for his strict punctuality and for arriving on a bicycle. The Regiment Sergeant Major RSM Ayling, was equally admirable as he would be found walking towards the drill square every morning even though he owned an impressive Ford car in those days. These examples stood me in great stead, for they helped me respect the values as much as the commitment to physical fitness in the Indian Armed Forces.

We also got pocket money of ₹ 30 per month, which was meant to supplement our diets. So, while the slightly richer and well-to-do boys managed to get some allowance from home, which enabled them to get better supplies and purchases, I chose to buy large quantities of cheap bananas from the canteen to fill up my stomach. Sometimes, a precious *samosa* was surreptitiously bought. On the lighter side, I attribute my deep love for the magnificent fried *samosa* to this golden period of my life.

The Army not only trained us in self-reliance, what is now called *atmanirbharta,* but also embraced the spirit of camaraderie and give and take. It was this beautiful paradox of independence and interdependence that made me fall in love with a regimented life far away from my own family. Cleanliness became the *sine qua non* of my life, while the pride in being a soldier became an integral part of my personality.

Friendships blossomed amidst the good and the tough times. Cadet G S Salaria was now a close friend, but we never forgot that we came together thanks to a precious pact that entailed assisting each other to get through cadet life. So, while I would help him brush up on academics and teach him the intricacies of the English language, he would toughen me up by teaching boxing and swimming. This teamwork worked miracles, and I began practising at night. The results were astounding as I started clearing swimming and PT Tests. He, too, began scoring respectably in his studies. It was a win-win.

As a boxer, I learnt that I was deadly with my left uppercut knockouts of my opponents. What an achievement it was to win the Light Heavyweight in Amateur Boxing and swim the three mandatory lengths with a heavy pack on. I was also a part of the Academy Boating Team, which won competitions at Peacock Bay. I equally enjoyed learning the Chinese Language from Professor Tagore.

Big Joe from Kumaon, another friend of mine, also joined our group, as did my pal Pramod Kapoor, who was later awarded the Sword of Honour. Shankar Roy Chowdhary, another dear coursemate from NDA, went on to become the Chief of the Army Staff. All these luminaries of today were mere teenagers obsessed with the thought of surviving a tough military training establishment with their self-belief and dignity intact. What actually happened was beyond our limited imagination as we not only made it but actually thrived in this nurturing environment that turned out to be a cradle of leadership. I remember one of the senior officers remarking that cadets should come to the academy even sooner to prevent them from being influenced by the ills of society. They did make men out of boys, rather officers and gentlemen out of teenagers who were unsure of their path.

And just like that, the tide began to turn and we turned seniors. The grand finale saw us participate and succeed in the dreaded Torna Camp in the last term when it was our team that won the arduous Chindits March in April 1956.

What had begun as a never-ending nightmare became a way of life for me. Not only was I getting stronger and fitter thanks to those innumerable front rolls and back rolls, which, quite unlike the delicious bread rolls that were sometimes served for breakfast, were not the slightest bit desirable, but I was also becoming wiser, more focused, more in control of my career and my life.

I was a senior for two years as Cadet 1242 of the first NDA 10th JSW Course once the NDA was formally commissioned as the first tri-service academy and we moved from Clement Town to Khadakwasla near Pune.

As I look back at those times, I also realise that this was the time I began to enjoy every activity, thus allowing the blossoming of a new chapter of cadet life. I got a lot of opportunities, and I took them all without fail. A lot of credit must go to the interest taken by the NDA Commandant, Major

General Enaith Habibullah and Mrs Hamida Habibullah, who managed to give a great boost to the Arts at the NDA. This allowed me to take on some great roles, one of them being the founder of the History Club, which started the interesting series called 'Facts of History Served with Spice of Life.' This caught the fancy of cadets and senior officers, who were happy to promote this popular club. Being a fan of literature and dramatics made me look forward to events where I could showcase my talent. Thus, a highlight moment that arrived for me was the 'Asia Awakes' pageant, which saw the participation of the Shakespeareana group from Delhi.

What a pleasure it was to be face to face with its elite director, none other than the man Geoffrey Kendall himself, whom I had briefly met during my Harcourt Butler days. Kendall was accompanied by his wife, Laura and daughters, Jennifer and Felicity. It was a dream come true to enact scenes from some of my favourite Shakespeare plays with the thespian himself. The glittering finale, which was organised at the huge amphitheatre at NDA, was everything I could ever imagine it to be.

I did not let go of opportunities to upgrade my dancing skills as I realised the importance of bringing a fine balance to our hard life through the joys of dancing. The credit for being a fine dancer, with a special talent for the waltz and the foxtrot, must be rightfully attributed to Mrs La Fontaine, who was married to Denis La Fontaine, the officer who went on to become Air Chief Marshal. While she passed this skill on to me, I not only reaped the benefits directly but also went on to pass it to junior cadets who would need all the help in preparing for the dance evenings with the girls from Wadia College. I fondly recall one such dance session where a nervous cadet repeatedly stepped on our instructor, Mrs La Fontaine's toes, while apologising profusely with the excuse, 'Pardon me,

Ma'am, I am just a starter.' Her quick-witted response became a classic joke in the academy as she remarked, 'I know you are a starter, but my feet are not your accelerator.'

Another memorable experience came with the staging of the famous play 'Witness for the Prosecution' which was adapted from a short story by Agatha Christie. This classic production was an opportunity to get better acquainted with stalwarts like Mrs La Fontaine and Mrs Ayling, wives of senior officers, who were avid theatre enthusiasts and under whose tutelage I learnt so much. For my role, I even learned the correct pronunciation and accurate usage of phonetics from Professor Dastur, which imparts authenticity to the play.

Not only were these shows a great hit, but they also gave me the thrill of a standing ovation, which was a much-needed validation of my talents, something I desperately needed to stay motivated. In fact, each of the four terms opened up new facets of my personality as I acquired multiple skills that contributed to making me a well-rounded cadet.

Excelling at riding gave me as much of a thrill as did the boxing practice. I remember having reached the finals of the 'Light Heavy Weight' category and facing Gentleman Cadet Manhas. The bout was never-ending as I kept up the tempo and the stamina despite bleeding from the nose. My competitive spirit would not allow me to pause or stop even though, as per points, I lost to Manhas. As a consolation prize, it was heartening to be commended by the coach as a good sport and be given the light-hearted title of the 'Best Loser' for my refusal to give up.

'When things get tough, I get tougher.'

This has been my motto, and I continue to relate to this feeling of fighting ferociously till the end, irrespective of the outcome. What a thrill it was, then and now, to see India's first

Prime Minister, Pandit Jawaharlal Nehru, taking the salute as my platoon marched by with military precision. I equally cherish the group photo with my coursemates, which has now found pride of place at the National Defence Academy at Khadakwasla and shows an unrecognisable young man seated ramrod straight in the third row. I was an excited 19-year-old who could not contain his joy when we passed out on 26 May 1956 from the Academy Drill Square, with the first termers manning the Flag Mast.

Soon enough, it was time to move to the prestigious Indian Military Academy at Dehradun, where I became a part of the Casino Company and where my Company Commander was Major Mike Skinner from the famous Skinner;s Horse. At the IMA, too, I was an active participant in the dramatics club, thus getting a chance to be a part of the production called 'Tons of Money' where my character paired opposite Mrs. Skinner, my Company Commander's wife.

My involvement with all these activities brought me rather close to my Company Commander, Major Skinner, who promised to make me a part of his Regiment. Alas, when the allotment of arms was being done, I was nowhere in the running. A disappointed me when asked to select any other arm had no choice but to turn to destiny.

True to the adage that 'When a door closes, a window opens somewhere, ' this news was heart-breaking only until the time that I learnt that I could join the Sikh regiment. My deep bond and spiritual connection with Punjab were best fulfilled by serving with the prestigious Sikh regiment. It was a decision that defined my future.

Nishchay Kar Apni Jeet Karon

I will win with my determination.

The Sikh Regiment Credo

1959

The Tigers

'Why is the 17 Sikh regiment referred to as 'The Tigers?'

This was a genuine and innocent query on the very first day of joining this regiment. It was prompted by a large signage with the words 'The Tigers' emblazoned on it as we walked into the main foyer of the Officer's Mess for dinner. My colleagues looked at each other and then at me before taking me on a walk-through along the walls of the Officer's Mess.

I was shown a slightly bent bayonet on one wall while, from the corner of my eye, I could not ignore the lifelike face of a tigress captured in a roar with its glossy skin sprawled all over the wall. It was a glorious, albeit an intimidating sight that only served to deepen the mystery.

It was only when I began perusing the numerous newspaper cuttings of the event that occurred in 1954 that I got some understanding of the courage and bravery of Sucha Singh, so much so that it continues to merit a prime place on the most prominent walls of the Officers' Mess till date.

Before I finished the tour, my colleagues began narrating the legend of *Havaldar* Sucha Singh, who was declared a hero and promoted to Lance Naik, for being singlehandedly responsible for the rechristening of the 17 Sikh regiment as the

Tiger Battalion since that fateful day in 1954.

I was particularly intrigued as I realised that it was Lt. Col. Shamsher Singh who was commanding the regiment at the time and that the battalion was at Shivpuri for an exercise.

'It began innocently enough when Fauja Singh, the staff at the Officer's Mess in Agra, set events in motion as he went deeper into the forest to collect firewood. This was when the tigress attacked Fauja Singh,' said my colleague.

The other officer added.

'He extricated himself, but in the melee, his turban disappeared. The injured sepoy was evacuated to the military hospital where he continued to lament the loss of his precious turban for days.'

I could believe it. Every true Sikh is deeply attached to his headgear.

He continued the story.

'Meanwhile, our decorated and devoted Commanding Officer was understandably concerned about the presence of a tigress in the vicinity. The situation was particularly delicate as the tigress had turned maneater. The action was a must to protect the officers and men. Two companies of the 17 Sikhs formed an assault line with the Commanding Officer's party in the centre. Bayonets were fixed on the Enfield .303 rifles and the assault commenced.'

I was on the edge of my seat. It is rightly said that truth can be stranger than fiction. When storytelling is as vivid as this one, even listening is visualising and is truly exhilarating.

'The tigress leapt out of the thicket and attacked the assault line. Sepoy Sucha Singh, who was directly in front, adopted the traditional bayonet fighting stance, meeting the tigress head-on with his weapon. As she lunged at him, he plunged his bayonet into her chest. While it was buried to the hilt, the momentum threw off Sucha Singh while his bayonet developed a 10-degree curve due to the impact with the tigress.'

My colleague paused to catch his breath after this passionate storytelling, which had all the ingredients of a thriller. The impact of this saga was hair-raising and I would not have even believed it had I not seen the bayonet as proof of the valour of our very own hero.

This was no urban legend but my rite of passage into understanding the bravery and heroism of the 'Tiger Battalion.' I was convinced that the people I would now be working with were special in every way and deserving of my complete loyalty and respect.

The more I read about my regiment, the more I understood them and connected with their ethos. Historically, too, the Sikhs were special. Beginning with the first Battalion of the Sikhs, which was the very first unit to be airlifted to Srinagar in the war of 1947-48 against the Pakistani forces at a time when I would have been barely ten years of age, I could feel the surge of pride at being part of such a hallowed institution.

What an impressive history the Sikh Regiment had! It was a testimony to the courage imbued in the Sikhs and I was proud to be a part of this regiment. *Nishchay Kar Apni Jeet Karon* was the magical mantra of the Sikh regiment and I believe it made them the formidable force they are. My heart skipped a beat while every pore of my skin surged with pride as the Regimental song was sung in its classic full-throated style.

My association with the Sikh regiment turned out to be a great learning period for me and the spiritual alignment that I already had with Punjab and the Sikhs was strengthened when I understood their ethos better. The principles of the Armed Forces, in general, and the Sikh battalion, in particular, resonated with the family values that were inculcated in me. A galaxy of young officers like Trevor Morlin, J C Joshi, Rajinder Dahiya and Soli Canteenwala, my companions in boxing, were my colleagues and compatriots as well as mentors and well-wishers. I was eager to imbibe all of these life lessons and become the best version of myself.

Duty always came before pleasure and yet we squeezed in brief periods of socialising before I was posted to Jammu & Kashmir at one of the toughest terrains. Called Nastachun Pass, which literally translates to 'Nose Cut', this mountain pass in Jammu and Kashmir connects Karnah tehsil of Kupwara district with the rest of the Kashmir valley. It is now referred to as the Saadna Pass and this is where we learnt the ropes of survival amidst challenging circumstances.

A different sort of growing up happened while I was posted at the Sikh Regimental Centre in Meerut. I was privileged to be under the guidance of the legendary Col. Shamsher Singh of the First Patiala Sikh, who joined the Sikh regiment in 1954 and eventually retired as Colonel of the Regimental Center. He was my mentor and Guru during those early years and I looked up to him for his humility, determination, bravery, and his righteousness. Known far and wide for his integrity and foresight, my commandant shared stories of the early days that would surprise any of us today. A sepoy told him that all the men were used to pitching in money at the rate of one *anna* per *jawan* to foot the personal club bill of their Oxford-educated Lieutenant Platoon Commander. When he refused to continue this outdated tradition, the men felt a sense of rejection, such was the extent of conditioning into slavery that the brave soldiers of that time were subjected to.

Another development that helped me mature was the arrival of my father, who had since retired and decided to make his home with me even though I was the youngest son of the family. He insisted on being with me and mentioned that he felt pride in being a part of the Armed Forces environment. This turn of events needed many logistical changes and I had to manage accommodation and other comforts for him.

Though *Bauji* did receive a modest amount as a pension and would never wish to burden me, money became tight for a bachelor like myself. My amateur attempts at proving my financial capability in providing him with the best quality of life ended badly as I began borrowing money from friends. What I considered confidential information eventually made its way to my Commandant, who, unfortunately for me, thought the worst. Assuming that I was either suffering from some addiction or was careless and undisciplined, he decided to rescue me from turning into a wastrel by taking control of my chequebook. He also gave strict instructions that I would only be allowed to issue cheques after giving a valid reason for its requirement. While this seemed like a harsh way to inculcate fiscal discipline, it worked in my favour. During the period that I was forced to write an application to be able to issue a cheque from my own earnings and for my own expenses, I became very organised and responsible.

What seemed like a punishment turned out to be one of the most valuable learnings, more so as the person responsible for this extreme step was the Sikh Regiment Commandant, Col. Shamsher Singh, the same man who led the attack that resulted in my regiment being called 'The Tigers?'

In this avatar, as my guru and mentor, he made me introspect on how much I needed every month for my expenses. By insisting that I needed his approval to use the money that I earned, he became a role model who helped me appreciate careful spending habits. I soon learnt to cut down on unnecessary expenditures. In fact, some of my prized possessions were made possible because of these values.

It was a proud moment for me when I became the owner of one of the best cycles at that time, a Raleigh with gears. They were bought in monthly instalments after due clearance from my Commandant. These were the formative years where every day was a learning and handling finances became my strength, helping me later in becoming an effective personal auditor.

My association with the Sikh Regiment has been beyond time and even my Armed Forces tenure. It has given me support through all stages of life and during the turning points of life like marriage, the time spent in forward areas to maintain peace on borders or when my family lived in separated family quarters. I love to flaunt that I am '18 till I die', that I will give my life for *Chhe* (Six Sikh Regiment) and that I am a 'Tiger' forever. The Sikh Regiment and my personal life have merged and blended as one.

It's Only Words
And Words are all I have
To Take Your Heart Away

Lyrics of the Song 'Words'

1962
Urmil

Exciting, glamourous, unpredictable, challenging…there is no end to the adjectives that I can use for my life in the Armed Forces. The only thing it could never be was boring. Given the nature of our work, which was mostly confidential and our frequent movements and hectic schedules, it was hard to make friends beyond the scope of military life. But it must be my destiny that I have always been a lucky charm in terms of friendships.

These were the 'swinging sixties' and I was a single officer with a desire to live life to the fullest. Fortunately, life presented me with unique opportunities to make friends for life in the time that I spent in Meerut.

I met Prabir Banerji, a young bachelor of medium height and slim built who belonged to the landed gentry of Meerut and lived at Begum Bridge in the heart of Meerut's business centre. Our first interaction was at the much-loved hub called the Wheeler Club which was situated just opposite Lal Quarters where I lived. Since their dance parties and events were legendary, I missed no opportunity to interact with the charming people who frequented it. In fact, I bumped into Prabir when both of us were busy trying out the latest dances with the young ladies. It was friendship at first sight.

He had a large residence cum commercial estate on the main road. Being the only son of his deceased parents, he lived by himself, though his older sister, who was married, resided in one of the adjacent bungalows. As the sole owner, he managed a large retinue of staff, which included a driver, a gardener, two housekeepers, and cleaning staff, all of whom had their quarters within this two-acre establishment. There was always an invitation to Prabir's Estate, where we not only enjoyed parties and dancing but also found time to indulge in literary pursuits. Over time, I began to spend every Sunday with Prabir when we bonded over books, life and spirituality.

As happens to all of us eventually, our family commitments inevitably supersede the fun and frolic that bachelors like us would be happy to forever indulge ourselves with. It was no different for us. It began with the most eligible bachelor of Meerut – my buddy Prabir. As marriage alliances started pouring in for him, the family zeroed in on a suitable girl, resulting in a visit to Benaras to meet her and her family.

Meena, the chosen one, was unanimously selected for her family background, her pristine beauty and her musical prowess. It is said that her suitors included popular film stars so Prabir was warned that his competition was tough. But Prabir was a prize, too, gifted in so many ways. He was well-to-do, highly educated, and an epitome of sophistication and charm to boot. It was a fairy tale wedding once my gentlemanly friend won over Princess Meenakshi.

While Prabir won over the delightful Meena, I scored my share of triumph by getting the love and affection of my new family while I was being taught how to wear a *Dhoti Kurta.*

As soon as we arrived in Benaras, we were blown over by the warmth of the hospitality that was accorded to us. As the person closest to Prabir, I was invited to be a part of all the ceremonies and proceedings like a true Brahmin. This meant that I was required to wear a *Dhoti* and sit cross-legged on the floor, something I had never done before, certainly not simultaneously.

In a series of hilarious incidents, I was amused to see the coy bride burst into delightful laughter at my awkwardness in the unfamiliar outfit that I had to wear, more so as I went through the harrowing experience of a slippery *Dhoti.* My soon-to-be *Bhabhi* decided to call me 'Prithi *Bhai'*, and the name stuck. I reciprocated by calling her 'Meena *Behen*.'

These memories continue to evoke nostalgia for a friendship so true and for the emotions so pure and deep that this bond of friendship continued even when Prabir was gone far too early. I continued to be Prithi *Bhai* for Meena and their son Soumitro, who became my godson. I could count on them and them on me at every stage of our lives.

Friendship was in abundance within the Army, too. Capt J M Mohan and Capt Ranbir Thapar from the Sikh Regiment became good friends of mine and Capt J M Mohan was even my double room partner as we shared accommodation.

It was a rather special moment when he managed to lay his hands on a second-hand Indian 5 HP Motorbike with hand gears and wide apart handles. It was truly a mean machine, but he could not manage it, attributing it to not being broad-shouldered enough. It was no surprise to me that I would be his designated driver. And so it was that I drove and he was pillion while we did some true-blue bike rides on the Meerut - Delhi highway at speeds that touched 100 kmph simply because we wanted to enjoy the fabulous coffee at the Gaylord Brasserie. Another time, the silencer fell off and we practically roared over the Meerut Mall Road with Mohan holding on to me for dear life. On that same occasion, we literally stormed into Prabir's Estate to get it repaired and were reprimanded by his wife for the mighty racket we were creating.

Some of my pals and I were close in literal terms as well as we had adjacent rooms that opened with a connecting door. One of them had a girlfriend at the time who often visited him from Delhi. I did hear that he planned to marry her, but I had never had an opportunity to meet her and as friends, we never interfered in each other's personal lives.

In an unfortunate circumstance, my friend's girlfriend, who we later learnt was clinically depressed, committed suicide. Her brothers cast aspersions on my poor friend and even on myself and came looking for him. It was a curious turn of events as they found me sleeping under a mosquito net in the summertime and, assuming that I was him, rudely woke me up and confronted me. Even though I was shaken up by this aggression, I sensed their grief and anger, kept my cool and clarified my identity while vouching for my friend's innocence. They were apologetic and later had a civil interaction with my pal, who was equally sad about this tragic loss.

This episode served as a wake-up call for him and for myself as we became more vigilant about our friend circle. None of us wanted to hurt anyone or get diverted from our professional and personal development.

And just when we thought matters could not worsen came the deadly riots in Meerut in October of 1961. I was given charge of the Begum Bridge Zone with our headquarters at the corner near Nishat Cinema. The supply of milk and vegetables was badly hit as curfew was declared, and I made every effort to have some delivered to the estate for my pal Prabir and his newly-wed wife, Meena *Behen*. On one occasion, I even managed to procure her favourite *kulche-chole* from the famous *nukkad wala* vendor, which she loved and missed.

Despite those moments of respite, these were truly terrible days and we were witness to many ugly clashes. Our soldiers were part of many flag marches that were designed to soothe the atmosphere and bring peace to Meerut. Be it the enemy or even the fractious forces within, the Army's role was vast and our requirements never eased; they just changed according to the circumstances. This assignment was difficult and yet satisfying, and I was gratified to be commended by my superiors.

Barely two months later, it was time to move once again. This time, I was to be a part of another historic moment because even after India achieved its independence from the British in 1947, Portugal refused to exit Goa, Daman,and Diu and dealt with the freedom struggle rather viciously. When diplomatic attempts failed, military action was the only option left.

I was fortunate to join a platoon of the 3rd Sikh regiment that went to Goa in December of 1961 for Operation Vijay for the liberation of Goa. We arrived by the military special train and participated in an operation that lasted barely two days with little opposition and negligible casualties. The results were glorious and when General Chaudhri, accompanied by Air Vice Marshal EW Pinto and Chief of Staff, landed at Goa and flew the tricolour on 19th December 1961, it was a memorable moment that came ten days after my 25th birthday. What a glorious birthday gift for me to be a part of such a historic event.

True to the Goan spirit, I brought back Wincarnis Original Tonic Wine to share and enjoy with my closest friends. Back in Meerut, it was time to celebrate over cocktails and dinner, but not without obtaining approval from Dr Chatterji, Prabir's brother-in-law. He even gave permission for Meena *Behen* to imbibe just a small amount of the precious wine, and this was what triggered the fun.

Being a first-time drinker, just a few sips were sufficient to intoxicate her. It began with her announcement that Prithi *Bhai* would look better clean-shaven, so she wanted to shave off my moustache. This started a hilarious chase where she ran after me with a pair of scissors and I fled the scene to avoid any mishap. The entire Estate rang with laughter and merriment as my friends teased me.

I, too, was considered of 'marriageable age' in my early twenties, and suitable alliances were suggested to my father. Prabir and Meena's marital bliss was infectious enough to rub off on me, and I, too, was amenable to the idea of marriage. My father insisted on a match within the *Panchjaati* (five castes) of the Punjabi Brahmin community and shortlisted the proposal from the Jaitly family settled in Amritsar.

I learnt of this alliance only when I was told that two gentlemen, Tara Chand Jhingan and Kirpa Ram Sharma (Kip as he was known), visited Meerut to 'see' me. Not being aware of their visit in advance, they had to return without meeting me as I was in Delhi at the time. It was then conveyed to me through my father that I must meet them in Delhi, so I suggested a meeting near Regal Cinema in Delhi, where I had gone to see a movie. After a brief cat-and-mouse game, we met each other in a very amiable way, and another meeting was fixed to finalise this matrimonial alliance.

It was August of 1962 when Prabir Banerji and Meena *Behen* accompanied my elder sister Krishna and me to Kwality Restaurant at Connaught Place in New Delhi to meet the bride-to-be and her family. I was disappointed. And with good reason. I did not get to meet the bride, so I was introduced to the bride's older sister instead. My friend teased me later, saying that I was expected to say yes just by looking at the sister, who was pretty enough. In those days, the bride and groom were rarely consulted, and they were much less expected to offer any opinion, so my expectation of a meeting was not given much importance.

Crestfallen, I returned to Meerut only to get the message that this was only a preliminary family meeting and that I would soon get an opportunity to meet my future wife in Amritsar. I felt a sense of elation. But when the moment arrived, I was nervous even though I considered myself rather forward and was hoping to not just be introduced but also have a conversation with her.

It brings a smile to my lips as I recall the image that still flashes in my mind's eye. In walked a tall, slim and beautiful girl wearing a simple Punjabi style *salwar kameez* with a dupatta draped demurely over her shoulders and her two hair braids framing her make-up free face. Her simplicity was charming, as was her demureness. To a young man like me, she looked no less than a film star even though she studiously gazed down.

The meeting was dreamy but also awkward as my sister insisted that I ask my bride-to-be some questions. I shook my head, making a choice not to interrogate her as I wanted to avoid saying or doing anything that could make her uncomfortable. It was love at first sight for me and nothing could spoil the sheer dreaminess of that moment. Even though we could hardly interact, given the conservative set-up and the presence of our families during the finalisation of this alliance, it went smoothly from there.

The only time she raised her eyes in a quick, sharp glance was when I stood up on her arrival in true Armed Forces tradition. This may have been a winning move from my end, but she looked surprised, more so when I waited for her to sit before I sat down. I thought I had impressed her, but during our honeymoon, she corrected my thinking process.

'I wasn't impressed. In fact, I was surprised by your unnatural behaviour. Why did you stand up as soon as I walked in? You looked over-eager and desperate.'

I could only laugh at the much-touted chivalry of the Armed Forces that insists that an officer stand up when a woman enters. The Amritsar ethos had clearly clashed with the British style etiquette, and I was misunderstood.

Our marriage was fixed for 7th September 1962. I, a 25-year-old commissioned officer of the Indian Armed Forces, was delighted to have found my soulmate in Urmil, a 19-year-old Bachelor of Arts graduate from Government College for Women in Amritsar.

A worry began to lurk somewhere in the back of my mind. No one in her family had any association with the Armed Forces, so how could she say yes to me without any understanding of life in the Army? Did she even know that war clouds lurked over the country? Was she prepared to go through the vagaries of living away from family when she agreed to marry an Army officer? These questions haunted me till my family allayed my fears, saying she would be looked after well. I pushed away all my concerns and got ready for the big day.

The marriage was a grand affair hosted by the bride's father, who charmed us with his hospitality and some excellent arrangements made for the wedding party at *Dhab Khatikan*. The icing on the cake was the presence of the Sikh Regimental Band with my fellow officers in attendance.

While everything about the wedding was magnificent, I did encounter some hiccups. A *ghodi* (mare) that had been arranged by my brother-in-law with the help of his friends who dealt with horses was clearly untrained to handle wedding festivities, and I was asked to be seated on the mare during the *baraat* (wedding procession) up to Katra Dulo. It turned out that this mare preferred to be free of any encumbrances that involved a groom and a merry crowd of dancing relatives. My mare was completely unpredictable as it turned frisky and excitable at some times and hesitant and reticent at other times, stopping at different places while shaking its head and neighing continuously. I needed all the horse-riding skills I had mustered in academy life to control it while protecting a bevy of laughing and dancing *baraatis* as well as my young nephew seated in front of me as my *sarbala.* When matters seemed to get out of hand, the horse attendant was chided by my father. This is when he murmured some words in the mare's ear to finally calm down my *ghodi.*

I was relieved to dismount safely and be welcomed at the bride's home. From then onwards, all the ceremonies proceeded as planned and we were soon a married couple, heading out in a taxi for Delhi's Ajmeri gate bus stand where we boarded a bus for Nainital and Ranikhet where we spent a week of honeymoon.

This was our time together and we made the most of it. We got to know each other better, we talked, we laughed and we utilised every moment to build a solid foundation for a brand-new relationship. Our stay at Nainital was particularly idyllic as we spent lazy days at the Kumaon Regiment Holiday Home. We then proceeded to Ranikhet, where we trekked and rode horses and I taught her how to play card games like Bridge. Not surprisingly, she mastered it and beat me at it.

On our return journey to Delhi, we travelled to Chandigarh to spend time with my eldest sister, Kaushalya *behenji,* my *Jijajee* Prof. PD Shastri, and their children. It was truly a grand reunion as their home had always been my refuge, my safe haven.

In a stroke of luck, I was fortunate enough to be posted with the 18 Sikh in Amritsar just after I got married and, as a bonus, it was Capt J M Mohan who was adjutant. This ensured that I would be in my wife's hometown, close to family support, and while at work, I could count on the support of my friend Mohan.

Urmil and I occupied our very first home in Amritsar - a well-appointed bungalow on the posh mall road where the next few weeks simply flew by as we savoured every moment of our newly married life.

Like all Army officers, I had the privilege of a buddy or *Sahayak* who would assist me in managing my home, my numerous uniforms and shoes. It was amusing to see Prem Singh explain the purpose of all these uniforms to my wife, who was thoroughly perplexed by this confusing rigmarole of different uniforms for different activities – be it office or training, games and recreation or socialising at the officers' mess. She wisely chose to focus on her own areas of expertise, while Prem Singh seemed to be happy to have his monopoly as far as I was concerned. *Bauji,* along with my youngest sister Rani, joined us in Amritsar. I am glad they did, as my country and my duty beckoned me.

It was time to pause marital bliss as news about Chinese soldiers launching an attack on all sectors of the border was confirmed. The country was at war.

When you go home, tell them of us and say, for your tomorrow, we gave our today

War Memorial Epitaph

1971
Chaos

It was on 20th October 1962 that the minor border skirmishes turned into a full-blown war, and artillery fire intensified in the North-East Frontier Agency (NEFA), bordering China and Bhutan. This attack overwhelmed the 7th Infantry Brigade, which was deployed on the Namka Chu River in the Western part of Arunachal Pradesh. A Chinese offensive was simultaneously launched in the Ladakh region. Chaos and turmoil raged, both in the country and in my mind.

While we were aware of tensions on the border, nobody, least of all the Indian leadership, imagined that China would attack. The Army was completely unprepared for this war. Amidst mounting losses, mobilisation commenced.

We believed China was our friend, so this seemed like a betrayal of the highest order. I felt betrayed, too. I was barely married a month and hadn't even got to know my wife well enough to say goodbye when my regiment was ordered to move to Bagdogra. My Commanding Officer even offered me the choice of staying back as I was recently married.

'But what was the right thing to do,' I wondered as I faced one of my biggest moral dilemmas. I reflected on the right course of action and concluded that my wife deserved far more. I had to make sure she would be safe, secure, and well looked after.

I was equally obsessed with being a part of this mission and proving my usefulness to my country and my people. Not only was I unafraid of war, I believed I was born to be a soldier. I would be devastated not to be a part of it.

But before serving the nation, there was something I needed to do immediately. It entailed completing a formality of signing my pay in Urmil's name. Once done, I was ready to move to the front and give it my best. We were scheduled to leave by train from Delhi the very next day when Urmil announced her decision to see me off at the Delhi Railway Station, from where I would be boarding the Military Special.

I was moved by her supportive acceptance, and suggested that she spend time in Chandigarh at my sister's house, where she would get the required guidance and support system to focus on her postgraduate studies. She agreed readily and began to pack her suitcase.

We arrived to see the Delhi railway station milling with people. Hundreds of young men in uniform were loading luggage onto the train while women and kids watched the pandemonium with worry writ large on their faces. Some of them could be seen sobbing silently, and some even wailed loudly as the sons or husbands bid goodbye and boarded the train.

Detached from the noise and commotion stood my young wife. She cut a lonely yet strong figure as she watched me board and then waved as the train glided past. I felt a pang as I whispered to myself.

'*Au Revoir,* my dearest Urmil, till we meet again.'

The train picked up speed. Her goodbye wave would haunt me that night as she turned into a speck while the train relentlessly chugged towards its destination.

Watching her poise and grace made me appreciate the role of the soldier's spouse. These unsung heroes of the Armed Forces also suffer pangs of war. It also reminded me of a strangely ominous and ironic conversation on our wedding night when I asked her the meaning of her name.

'My father named me Urmila from the Ramayana, but my mother was against this name and really worried for me.'

'Why? It's a nice name. Urmila was Sita's sister and Lakshmana's wife, right?' I queried

'Yes, that's what my mother worried about. Lakshman accompanied Lord Rama in exile and stayed away from Urmila for 14 years. My mother worried that the name could bring the same fate to me,' she laughed at the absurdity of her mother's objection.

I felt a sense of foreboding. A *Fauji* like me would be forced to abandon her to focus on his duty and mission. This was unfair on Urmil, I reflected, but I was blessed to have a supportive spouse back home.

Thoughts of my wife on the one hand and my duty on the other continued to intrude on my sleep till we reached our destination. Barely had we settled down, and I received one of the biggest surprises of my life when I was told that there was a visitor who wanted to meet me. I could hardly believe my eyes as I saw the smiling, cherubic figure of my wife's only brother.

'*Bhape!*' I shouted as I rushed to embrace him. My dearest *Saala* (wife's brother), the ever-devoted Kailash, had arrived late at night at the flea-infested Army base on Sevok Road, Siliguri, simply because he was unable to make it in time to see me off at the Delhi railway station.

How he managed to catch a train and then follow the Army convoy all the way to this remote base while struggling with directions and requesting help from the Mechanical Transport Section continues to be a mystery. Suffice to say, it strengthened my faith in the family values that made the Jaitley's some of the most affectionate people on this earth. I was overwhelmed by the love that drove him to undertake such an adventurous trip. A trip that required a local ferry in areas where not even a bridge could be found across the river. He barely stayed for a few hours before taking the dangerous trek back while I couldn't help but reflect on the things one can do for one's family. My wife and her siblings would move heaven and earth for each other's sake and they proved it time and again. I felt blessed to be a part of their family.

War times are never easy and what followed in the next few weeks was nothing but a tragic debacle. Indian soldiers were heavily outnumbered by the Chinese troops. And we were under-equipped in every way. Our troops wore canvas shoes, the type school children wear for their PT. If this is what my jawans are wearing, what chances do we have to even get a grip on those treacherous borders? We also had vintage weapons and our clothing was completely climate inappropriate. Yes, this onslaught hit us like a sledgehammer, and yet, despite the odds, the limited ammunition, the inclement weather and the poor intelligence reports, Indian troops fought valiantly and went down fighting.

While these were turbulent times, they passed soon enough. China withdrew unilaterally, but the war came with plenty of harsh lessons. Some of what we have learned and others that still need to be learnt and implemented. The Armed Forces have to be nurtured and built so that they can adequately protect the nation. The sacrifice of so many of our brethren was a humbling experience, and even sixty years later, those losses continue to haunt many of us who were a part of this war. More importantly, it makes us cherish peacetime as I resolved to spend quality time with my family.

Barely had I returned that I received my posting orders to Station Headquarters in Beas. This was great news. My wife and I were both delighted to move into our accommodation in a vast palace perched atop a hill near the Beas Rail Road Bridge. Popularly known as the White House, it was also situated at a convenient distance from Amritsar. We had all the family support that we could hope for and being a spacious bungalow, my wife and I could get all the privacy that a young couple craved for.

While at Beas, I bought a second-hand scooter so we could visit Amritsar often. My father-in-law, *Pappaji,* even gifted us a cow that gave enough milk for all of us with enough to spare. My wife and I enjoyed playing badminton with family and friends, while my own father, *Bauji,* would often invite his friends from the Railways. We had frequent visitors, including Mr Rishikesh, father-in-law of my sister Santosh, who would arrive by the morning train from Amritsar and discuss everything under the sun and we would insist he carry fresh produce from our huge vegetable garden.

This idyllic existence was also a bane for us as we were too far from medical assistance on that stormy night when Urmil had a spontaneous abortion. As she bled, panic-stricken, we rushed to the closest village dispensary at Dhilwan, across the river. The dilation and curettage procedure (D&C) performed to clear the uterine lining was conducted by the light of a lantern while I stood outside the makeshift operation room praying fervently for my young wife's wellbeing. It was a harrowing time for both of us. We lost our baby that fateful night. For the next few months, my wife and I grieved the loss. I also thanked my stars that my wife returned to better health soon.

Did I mention that just after marriage as we were returning to Amritsar from New Delhi, I had a vision of three little girls playing in my garden? I remember how Urmil laughed when I shared this vision with her. I somehow knew this was a portent of things to come. I was surely meant to father daughters.

When one door closes, another opens. It was towards the end of the year of 1963 that happiness traipsed into our household. Once again, we discovered that Urmil was pregnant. This time around, I wanted to take no chances and neither did her doctor, who urged her to be meticulous with her visits to the hospital. Much as I wished to be by her side, the call of duty beckoned once more. I was deputed to Srinagar Station Headquarters and agreed with Urmil's father's request that she move to her parental home for the delivery. It is quite another matter that the delivery happened at home with a midwife in attendance, despite my requests that she go to the hospital. Fortunately, all went well and I heaved a sigh of relief when the good news of her birth on 27th August 1964 came by telegram.

Our firstborn was a daughter. The first of the *Teen Deviyan* had arrived as predicted by my vision. I sent out a prayer of gratitude. I was so impressed by the name given by Pandit Jawaharlal Nehru to his daughter Indira I added the suffix 'Priyadarshini' to Ritu, the name my wife and I had decided before she was born.

It was so thrilling to have this feeling of becoming a father that I wanted to celebrate and mark this moment in a unique way. I made a wager with my colleague Capt Chadha from the Engineering branch, that we would visit Lord Shiva all the way to Amarnath at Anantnag, Pahalgam, in the erstwhile Jammu and Kashmir, returning nonstop to Srinagar. He accepted and off we went by jeep to Chandanwari, carrying our belongings, *pitthu* style, on our shoulders.

What an exhilarating celebration that turned out to be. When I go back in time, I can still taste those mouth-watering, piping hot, crisp *paranthas* served by a benevolent Sikh as we prepare to climb Pissu Ghati to reach Shesh Nag. There was an atmosphere of pure bliss as he served us lovingly, making sure we had our fill of a delicious repast, which cost us a mere one rupee per *parantha.* We followed it up with sweet milky tea before we commenced our journey once again. As we continued running down Panchtarni, we stopped at Bakerwals for hot milk and then sped on towards the holy *Shivling.* Dusk fell and the skies turned pink and we spotted a pair of snow-white doves. This was the kind of sign I was looking for and it heralded peace and harmony and a healthy wife and daughter back home. I felt blessed. After offering prayers to *Bholenath,* we returned to Bakerwals for a night stay.

The next morning, we began trekking back to Srinagar. This time around, my mind was fixated on my wife and newborn daughter and I craved to go home. Leave was granted within the month and we could finally celebrate as a family. Her birth turned out to be the best time for a reunion with family and friends, as Prabir and Meena visited us with their own newborn son, Soumitro.

For the soldiers of the Indian Army, the simple pleasure of being surrounded by family is temporal. But these memories are not. We need a surfeit of such moments to survive the inevitable separation when we are far away from our loved ones.

As war clouds began gathering, it was time to defend the nation once again. The designated key to the proverbial lock of the Indo-Pakistan War of 1965 was Codeword Banner.

For me, this was personal. It was a war from home. Meanwhile, I had just received posting orders to Jalandhar, where I would be joining as General Staff Officer (GSO) Grade 3 to XI Vajra Corps along with four other General Staff Officers. We were briefed by none other than the big man himself, Lieutenant General Joginder Dhillon, the 6 feet 3-inch-tall colossus who was our Corps Commander.

General Jogi Dhillon briefed Balwant Singh Bains, Balbir Singh Lamba, P K Java and myself in the presence of Brigadier P.S Grewal, BGS and Lt Col Chhajju Ram, GSO 1. As preparations picked speed, we were confident that victory would be ours.

On the 4th of September 1965, amidst heavy air bombing at Wagah by the Pakistan Army, I was deputed to give the 'Banner' to 15 Division GOC at the forward base. The plan was to attack the very next evening.

I stopped to visit my wife's home at *Katra Dulo* on the way back to Rayya and asked the ladies and children to leave immediately for Jalandhar and occupy the house that we were allotted near Lovely Restaurant, where my wife, my father and my barely one-year-old daughter would be by themselves in my absence.

I was as concerned for her family as for mine, more so due to rumours and reports about Pakistan being hell-bent on cutting off Punjab and Kashmir from India. Sending her family members to Jalandhar was more for my peace, and in retrospect, it turned out to be an unnecessary exercise, but it put my mind at ease.

I was a witness to the fierce 3 Jat attack on Batapore, Lahore, which was led by Major General Niranjan Prasad, GOC, 15 Infantry Division, by crossing Ichhogil Canal (BRB) with Col. Desmond Hayde. By the evening of 6th September, they had reached within striking distance of Lahore and then came the devastating Pakistan Air Force Sabres attack, which forced them back.

At this point, we were not just the representatives of General Joginder Dhillon at Corps Headquarters, but also his eyes and ears as we dashed to and from the war zone on all four axis (Amritsar-Lahore, Khalra-Burki-Lahore, Khemkaran-Kasur-Lahore and Fazilka) into Pakistan in jeeps fitted with powerful wireless sets while reporting on all events for necessary action.

On the night of 5th September 1965, just two days before my 3rd wedding anniversary, India had responded on all four axis in a master counterstroke to Pakistan's Grand Slam on Chhamb to cut off Kashmir from the country. It was a massive miscalculation on the enemy end that India would not cross the International Border after the massive artillery at Chhamb attacked our air bases in Kashmir. The armour operations by 9 Horse on the main defences and flanks forced Pakistan armour to attack tanks and anti-tank weapons on the 6th and 7th of September, destroying their 10 Cavalry.

On 10th September, Pakistan 1 Armoured Division and 4 Armoured Brigade were defeated by the use of terrain. Generals Jogi Dhillon and Harbaksh Singh, straight-talking professional soldiers of the Sikh Regiment, had averted the Pakistan breakthrough across the Beas.

The part played by the two armoured regiments of Bharat Force sealed the fate of the enemy. General Jogi Dhillon, the Vajra Corps Commander, deputed me and GSO 1, Lt Col Chajju Ram, to rush to the Dera Baba Nanak Brigade, even though one span of the DBN Bridge had been blown.

It was a dashing action when the GSO I and GSO 3 assumed command over Kasoval and DBN enclaves. This was a strategic command exercised by the XI Corps Commander by changing local divisional and brigade commanders and sticking to the maintenance of aim. Khemkaran was overwhelmed and the horseshoe of armour and infantry anti-tank guns destroyed enemy Patton tanks, creating a graveyard of the most modern US tanks rolling out of Pakistani yards.

Maj Gen Mohinder Singh took over on 9th Sept 1965 while losses continued to mount. On 22nd September, 3 Jat of the 54-brigade captured Dograi and by the time the war ended, they had lost almost 500 officers and men with over 1500 wounded, but they also won 3 Mahavir Chakra and 4 Vir Chakra and numerous commendations for their valour.

The war finally came to an end on 23 September 1965 and that same year, I turned 29 years of age. Being a part of such an important war mission influenced me immensely. I had seen fear and worry, bloodshed and death, but I also witnessed sacrifice and valour, bravery and camaraderie and that strengthened my resolve to continue on this path while proving myself worthy of the Armed Forces.

It is said war changes you. On the one hand, you are numb and on the other, you are over-sensitive, and both these events occur at the same time. It also made me realise the significance of steadfastness even during the most difficult times because even when defeat stares you in the face, staying cool can turn the tide.

In 1966, I was in command of the B Company of 18 Sikh and posted at Bikaner, where the Durand Cup footballer, Lt Col PC (Chhottu) Sen, was my Commanding Officer. He generously arranged for one of the vacant palace houses to be utilised by us. This huge house, complete with wine cellars and poultry pens, where Chottu's poultry and turkeys were also housed, became our rented home for some time. My daughter was especially thrilled with the turkeys and we began a delightful period of domestic bliss in a palatial home with birds and animals for the company.

In 1967, the regiment moved to Harsil in Uttarkashi under the command of Lt Col Arvind Gopal Inamdar (whose son joined the Navy and was known to my son-in-law), and he moved my company to Nelang Valley bordering Tibet. Two companies of ITBP and Intelligence Detachment were also located with us. These were tough times as we were close to the disputed Sino-Indian Line of Actual Control (LAC).

My wife stayed in Amritsar for the delivery of my second daughter in 1968. At the time, I was at Joshimath praying at the shrine of Badri Nath. A little over a year later, in November of 1969, my youngest daughter was born. I prayed at the head of the Ganga River at Gomukh and felt fulfilled. My family was complete.

As a next step, I developed a passion for qualifying for the Defence Services Staff College Entrance Examination at Wellington, Coonoor. Me and my colleague Balwant Singh started preparations that bore fruit later. Having passed her Bachelor of Arts, my wife Urmil decided to join in to complete her Bachelor of Education studies. This was also the beginning of tough times. Health-wise, I became seriously ill with food poisoning at Nelang. When matters got out of hand, I was airlifted to the Military Hospital and, after a month-long stint in recovery, granted leave to recuperate at home. From this time onwards, it was my wife Urmil who undertook a strict regimen of food and milk diet without salt for two months to heal the ulcer caused by food poisoning. She decided to have the exact same food despite my protests. It was her perseverance, prayers and sacrifice that helped me recover. I am eternally grateful to her till today.

This was a crucial juncture in my career as it was time to prepare for my studies. For the Armed Forces, the 'Staff College' is one of its most prestigious appointments and I put my heart and soul into the preparation. Urmil, too, was preparing for a Bachelor of Education (B. Ed) to be able to pursue a career as a school teacher. We rented a small house where Urmil's step-sister brought fresh food and looked after our children. Our *Tapasya* and commitment and those of our immediate family paid off in December 1970 when the results were declared. We were both successful.

Preparations began for the big move to Wellington, near the Nilgiris, in Tamil Nadu, for the 26th Defence Services Staff College Course from 1st January 1970 to 27 December 1970. I moved my entire family for a year to the verdant environs of Wellington, along with a nanny who cared for my young daughters. It turned out to be such a glorious time, both professionally and personally.

This one-of-a-kind joint services institute gives training to all three services and officers from friendly foreign countries. This diversity provided for the best quality training in a rich and stimulating learning environment. After the successful completion of the year-long Staff College Course on 27 December 1970, it was time to move once again.

This time around, I was posted at the Army HQ as Deputy Assistant Quartermaster General 3 for the Western Sector in the Department of Operation Logistics at New Delhi. A new phase of life had begun. We rented a floor at Green Park Extension and my daughters began their first sojourn in New Delhi, the place where I was born and grew up. We began following a comfortable work-life balance with my family and work. And yet, peace continued to elude us.

War clouds were looming once again. It was the December of 1971, and the liberation of Bengal was in the offing with a massive holding operation on the Western Front. Brigadier Chacko Uthup was the Brigadier Quartermaster at the Army Headquarters, where I conducted daily briefings on war preparations. On one such occasion, Brigadier Chacko asked me if I wanted to go as second in command at a crucial sector and I immediately volunteered my services. To my disappointment, the office of the Chief of Army Staff turned it down as I was part of the core team that had not completed the mandatory one year.

I persisted. 'I am a soldier who was trained for the battleground and I am not ready to sit back just yet,' I pleaded.

They relented, and I received my posting orders from *Chhe* Sikh - the battalion that was assigned the task of holding a feature, which was the key to our defences in this sector. The Commanding Officer of the *Chhe* Sikh Regiment was the legendary Lt Col Kashmiri Lal Rattan at Poonch, who welcomed me in style.

'*Tu Kaun? Pirthee?*' He delivered his opening line in friendly Punjabi.

We hit it off straight away.

Commissioned in 1955 in the 4 Sikh Battalion at Ambala, Lt Col Rattan joined *Chhe* Sikh at Meerut Cantt on the re-raising of the unit in 1962. In the coming days, I was witness to his exemplary leadership on multiple occasions.

For now, it was a waiting game. At 3 pm on 3rd December 1971, when the Quarter Master, Captain Chanan Singh, raised his glass of scotch whiskey, we heard loud blasts.

'Road Blasting,' said Chanan.

'Medium Guns,' I responded.

I was right. The Indo-Pak war has begun.

On the evening of 3rd Dec 1971, Pakistan launched pre-emptive strikes on 11 airfields in Northwest India, including Agra. The Pakistan Airforce flew over Poonch to bomb the Srinagar Air Base. The bold plan for the capture of Poonch was hatched by Pakistan a few months earlier as they visualised establishing a corridor along the ceasefire line by capturing the defended localities on Shahpur and Danna features and at Guterian, along the Darangla nullah, about six to nine kilometres north and northeast of Poonch town.

The elements of the 3 J&K Militia occupying the Thanpir feature were moved in the early part of the night to reinforce Shahpur and Guterian localities before the troops ordered to relieve them could reach the area. The 9 POK battalion consequently found the Thanpir feature unoccupied except for a few administrative personnel whom they murdered brutally. When the relieving troops arrived at Thanpir, they were surprised by the Pakistanis already in occupation and suffered heavy casualties. The conditions at Thanpir were chaotic. The commanding officer and his medical officer were killed, the battery commander in support had taken over, and the mere fact that the routes behind were insecure and the possibility of a linkup remote had caused demoralisation all around.

It took time, but we consolidated. I was issued a pistol and along with Sepoy Magar Singh, Chanan and I proceeded towards the bunker in the base. So effective was the carpet shelling that some bunkers were pierced and a number of men killed.

From December 3, 1971 to December 6, 1971 the enemy launched a series of fierce attacks against the defended area. Early next morning, we laboured up in a one-tonner on the narrow road to Madari Ridge amidst enemy shelling and somehow survived it. Lt Col Rattan displayed conspicuous bravery and exemplary leadership as he defended the strategically important town of Poonch against a numerically superior Pakistani force in a battle that was fought hundreds of kilometres from Bangladesh. His uncanny sense of figuring out that the war cries they heard were not two separate battalions but the same contingent with Sunni and Shia attacking troops turned out to be the most crucial information that created confidence. Being experienced enough to know Pushto and the thought process of the attacking Baluchis of 5 Frontier Force, 7 POK and 51 Punjab, he succeeded in deceiving them into attacking counter-penetration points that were not held. I was inspired by the bravery and strategic thinking of Lt Col Rattan, who positioned himself in the most threatened locality, and unmindful of the heavy enemy shelling and small arms fire, moved from bunker to bunker, encouraging and inspiring his men to beat back the enemy attacks.

These gallant actions earned the unit numerous laurels, including the Theatre Honour of Jammu and Kashmir and Battle Honour 'Defence of Poonch 1971'. Lt Col Kashmiri Lal Rattan was awarded the Maha Vir Chakra for his courage, leadership and dedication to the service, and *Chhe* became legendary for his courage. This goodwill continued even later in life on the Burma Border in Nagaland in 1976 when I was the Commanding Officer of the Tigers. Being an integral part of the famous 1971 war, which is widely acknowledged as a shining example of the courage and resilience of *Chhe* Sikh in the 'Battle of Poonch,' is one of my finest moments even till today.

However, as much glory war brings, it devastates far more. I had left behind my wife, three little girls and my father and was always worried about their welfare. This time around, our families were exposed to the fear and helplessness that war creates among the civilian population. My family went through uncertainty every single day that I was away. Urmil later described how the air was rent with sharp whistles and sirens as she crouched near the transistor to listen to the latest updates on All India Radio. My little girls would help their mother paste black paper on window panes to block out the lights and would voluntarily switch off the lights when sirens sounded. When I narrated stories about the regiment's valour, they joined me in the war cry of the Sikhs.

Jo Bole So Nihaal,
Sat Sri Akal'

The one who takes His name, is the one who has it all.

Sikh War Cry

Full many a flower is born to blush unseen,
And waste its sweetness on the desert air.

— Thomas Gray, An Elegy Written in a Country Churchyard

1974
North East

Dhana Sagar, in Madhya Pradesh was our next location. The *Chhe* moved into the old barracks without proper accommodation. As always, I made the most of my time with family, teaming up with Col Harnam Dev Kohol and his wife and visiting Sagar for movies and entertainment along with Urmil and my three daughters.

In those days, even though hunting was forbidden, some officers continued to go on a *Shikar* and shoot antelope, a distasteful practice for which the officer was admonished.

It was from Dhana that we moved to Ramgarh in 1974 when I assumed command of 17 Sikh, the battalion in which I was commissioned. This was a singular honour that resulted in much celebration. For me, it was a double honour as it meant command of the unit that I was commissioned in and a move from glorious *Chhe* to the brave *Tigers*. The tigress skin and the bent bayonet continued to have pride of place in recognition of the famous episode that occurred during an exercise in Madhya Pradesh when Sepoy Sucha Singh bayoneted the man-eating tigress. My daughters loved hearing the story repeatedly.

Our train reached Ramgarh railway station, a POW camp on the banks of the Swarnarekha river on 2 April 1974, where Col. D N Tankha, his wife Deepa and the officers, JCOs and men of the unit gave us a rousing welcome.

As the first lady of the Regiment, Urmil began taking on a much larger role in the Army Welfare Wives Association. Compassion and care came quite naturally to her, as did the subject of children's education. She started the 'Tiger Cubs' School for children of the area while supervising and expanding on the vocational training opportunities that helped empower the Army wives. Her dedication to this cause (AWWA or Army Wives Welfare Association) was so complete that she would visit the hospitals to support young wives during the birth of children and through any illnesses. These responsibilities were completely voluntary and came from her heart.

Brigadier Mazumdar and Major General Kulkarni were the Brigade and Division Commanders, respectively. A battle game was carried out on the banks of the Swarnarekha River to exercise assault across minefields and canals.

The Tiger Battalion was in the lead, and a device with a small anchor was thrown into the minefield and pulled back to clear any mines. One of my stalwarts, Sepoy Darbara Singh, had thrown the dragnet and pulled it back quite effortlessly when Gen Kulkarni decided to ask him this question.

'*Agar gadda hua to kaise clear karega?*'

(How would you clear it if there were a ditch here?)

Without a second's delay, he piped up.

'*Ay kam to tera hou?*'

(That would be your job)

There could have been no better example of the simplicity and straightforward nature of the Sikh than this innocent answer.

There was a stunned silence in the dead of the night before the riverfront came alive with the guffaws of the General. This 'Tiger' remained unfazed even as the game was declared a success. The 17 Sikh continued to prove themselves in subsequent battles.

Another historic movement that happened in my tenure was when the entire regiment shifted base in a 'special' train.

This was a major logistic exercise and needed immaculate planning and execution as everything from men, equipment and stores was loaded and stacked methodically on the wagons. This includes the people and the heavy equipment that included ammunition. As families were also being moved in the same train and we would be spending a few weeks on this special train, it became a self-contained city with its own unique character.

Vehicles were loaded onto special open wagons lashed by strong chains so that the heavy load did not shift during the movement while hectic preparations were afoot in the pantry wagon that would be catering for food for everyone on board. This was clearly one of the most integral parts, as feeding the battalion was a huge task and needed detailed planning. While pride of place in open wagons was reserved for our heavy weapons that braved the elements, equal importance was accorded to a small compartment that was transformed into the unit Gurudwara along with our *Granthi,* who would pray for our protection, especially during this move.

Our special train was commanded by an Officer in-charge Train (OC Train) and assisted by a Train Adjutant and duty officers/JCOs as per roster. As Commanding Officer, my compartment had all the facilities for me and my family, while the other first-class wagons were occupied by the Majors,

Captains, Lieutenants and JCO's as per seniority.

The Officers' Mess coupe was most sought after during the journey and assorted beverages were served after sunset to those not on duty that night.

Maintaining discipline and ensuring security of the men and equipment on the train was my main task, but also a collective responsibility which was led by the Officer in Command of the Train. It was he who would order halts for meals, daily ablutions and security checks by staying in direct communication with the train's engine driver and guard at all times.

As our train traversed through verdant climes and picturesque settings, there were requests to stop so the families could enjoy these picnic spots. At this time, the regiment cooks would set up makeshift kitchens and delicacies were churned out as snacks. This move turned out to be a delightful experience for the families and one that they cherish to date.

After another short stay with family, I was posted to a forward area in Nagaland where ambushes and skirmishes were daily occurrences. The hatred for the Army and the Sikhs was such that our *jawans* were often targeted and killed. This was a war to win hearts and it took all our effort to get them to trust us. But once they did, there was no looking back.

It was my pledge that none of the men ever take advantage of the local women and treat them with utmost respect. We allowed the locals to see the integrity of our intent without compromising on our professionalism as soldiers. This needed a balancing act, which finally proved to them that we were soldiers with both strength and soul. We also set up the first of the *Lavanya* Schools for children of the region. The word *Lavanya* was dear to me and the words from 'Elegy in a country churchyard' came alive when I saw the innocence of the children of the school. Urmil was a huge support in training the teachers with her Teacher Training skills.

It was the beginning of a new reputation for my soldiers and for myself. The result of this experiment in sensitisation created such a positive vibe while giving us much appreciation. The change in attitude and morale was so palpable that General Uppal commended my role and suggested I visit Manipur which too was up in arms. It was a game changer in Manipur and we decided to supply free salt to everyone and sensitise the officers and men to treat them respectfully. Even though this meant that I had to travel a lot, it was a fulfilling and productive period and I called it the war to win hearts.

On the personal front, I battled serious health issues. It began in Nagaland and was at the height of insurgency. Living in inhospitable climes and eating possibly spoilt tinned food caused such a violent illness that it became a matter of life and death. By this point, I had managed to have a real bond with the locals and when I was ill, they prayed to their own Gods for my health. I was carried to the nearest hospital in a *Palki* and finally airlifted to the hospital, where my stomach was flushed repeatedly. After spending a month in a hospital, I was finally declared out of danger. I was allowed to recuperate at home, where Urmil looked after me and nursed me back to health.

My next move with family was to Miransahib in Jammu, where I was appointed Deputy Brigade Commander under Brigadier Mahajan, who was the Brigade Commander.

Just as life was becoming more peaceful and settled, we faced another setback as this became the last posting with my dearest father, *Bauji,* who passed away in 1978. Urmil was eternally grateful to *Bauji* for his contribution to our family and was grateful that he only moved on once he was satisfied that his son was back home. This was some kind of divine providence that protected me and my family.

With my father gone, I had no reason to shy away from my household responsibilities and began performing them far more diligently. My three daughters were growing up and my wife and I needed to work as a team.

In 1979, I moved to Secunderabad to the 54th Division as Col. Q under the General Officer Commanding, General Rai. My wife and I have had the most cordial relations with all our bosses and colleagues, but in this case, we drew a blank. The General and his wife lived in a world of their own and we were placed in the most challenging situations while dealing with their expectations. I felt torn with the weight of the moral dilemmas that involved fulfilling the expectations of my boss, which were often opposed to the values that I believed in.

For some time, these dilemmas haunted me and I worried about the situation. It was my innate spirituality that helped me see the true path. I was reminded of the scriptures that urge us not to worry or even attempt to find retribution. Karma would find its way in its own time and justice would be served. But in the meantime, I was expected to toe the line without questions.

While I did my best to ignore the misappropriations and anomalies, two courts of inquiry held in 1982 and 1983 investigated the very same issues. When it was proven that the General and his wife accepted costly mementoes and overcharged their own officers to buy her paintings, a court martial was ordered. In a turning of tables, General Rai called to request me for a positive testimony.

It was at this time that the teachings of my spiritual mentor, *Swami* Sangdhar Das ji, came to my aid. He quoted the Bhagwad Gita as he reminded me that ' *Nishkam Karma or Karma Yog* is the easiest way to reach your goal.'

I would only side with the truth; I reflected even as his request took me back to the time when he left no stone unturned to isolate me and my wife as we did not indulge his whims. Another life lesson was there for us to imbibe. When the tide turns, no one is spared. Practising humility even when we are in positions of power or influence is the only way to maintain the officer-like qualities that the armed forces inculcate.

We also came back from Secunderabad with some beautiful memories. This place was just the right one for my daughters to shine as they excelled in academics as much as in the fine arts. As a family, we had the best time as we explored the city, socialised at the popular RSI club, enjoyed fish tikkas at Tank Bund and regularly visited the charming Birla Mandir atop the hill. Our palatial bungalow hosted fine parties and our relatives and friends visited us often.

The girls were growing up and they looked up to me to fulfil their dreams and ambitions. When I realised that my eldest daughter, while academically brilliant, loved to dance, I enrolled her in Kathak classes, where she made the most of her innate talent. My middle daughter loved to read and write and I encouraged her as much as I could, giving her writing tips, and enrolling her at the Amruthavani communications centre. In my youngest, I discovered an artist who loved to draw and paint. These were precious moments that brought us closer as a family. Life was looking up once again.

From 1981 to 1986, I was posted back to my hometown in a coveted position in the Ministry of Defence in the Directorate of Public Relations. This was a precious learning opportunity that resonated with my future plans of continuing as a defence correspondent post-retirement. The settling phase in Delhi was challenging as we were confined to one of the smallest transit accommodations on Curzon Road. A place that my resourceful wife turned into a much-loved home.

It took us over a year to manage to move into the 'A' type house in Sardar Patel Marg, which was a rapidly expanding area in the 1980s, in preparation for the Asian Games. This was our home for four years, and being part of the Directorate of Public Relations was an opportunity that I made the most of.

Working at the Ministry of Defence came with its own share of privileges and challenges. In many ways, it was a dream job for me and I loved the interactions, the press releases and press conferences, the media briefings and the sheer learning in the company of some of the greatest.

I remember when Principal Information Officer Lazarus and I went by the Army helicopter to Jessami to try the techniques we had developed to get closer to the insurgents. I got other opportunities to explore my own talents as a writer and editor with the monthly journal called *Sainik Samachar* and by anchoring the weekly programme on All India Radio and *Doordarshan,* which was called *'Sainikon Ke Liye.'* Being in the PR department of the Ministry of Defence came with a lot of privileges. As part of the board that censored films with any Armed Forces connection, we were exposed to myriad forms of art. This was also a great opportunity for me to be a part of the team that approved any military sequences from films like *Razia Sultan* and *Silsila,* among others. My family enjoyed the privilege of attending film premieres and fancy events and were exposed to privileges which were in stark contrast to the frugality with which a soldier lives. Times were changing and this blissful period ended in 1984 when we went from guts and glory to blood and gore. I not only witnessed it all but **observed it at close quarters and lived to tell the tale.**

Ik Onkar,

Satnam,

Karta Purakh

There's only one God, his name is the only truth

Guru Nanak Dev

1984
Amritsar

Urmil and I had a special affinity with Amritsar. Having physically resided in the city for the first 19 years of her life, her bonding was understandable, but mine was inexplicable, though no less deep. I may not have lived in Amritsar long enough, but thanks to the family connection, I was a regular visitor and shared a spiritual bond with this city, which was deep and true.

One of my biggest connections to the city was the Pandit Baij Nath (PBN) School, which was founded by my grandfather, the legendary Pandit Baij Nath and managed by my uncle Pandit Ram Nath. It was a physical link that established our legacy. Every time we visited the school, our father would show us the names engraved on that family tree that documented this connect. This bond became stronger and dearer after I met Urmil.

Post-marriage, the Amritsar visits inevitably began from *Katra Dulo,* where a cycle rickshaw would take us through the maze of the alleys and *gullies* (by-lanes) that made up my wife's family neighbourhood. The moment we spotted the corner temple with the genial figure of Lord Hanuman in flaming orange, we knew it was time to disembark and walk the final stretch to their traditional home. Her pandora's box of memories would come tumbling out as we arrived there.

And then there was the family temple nearby where I got the opportunity to connect with the radiant *Swami* Sarangdhar Das, the person who became my spiritual mentor and soul friend. Why would a young man of 16 years of age who hailed from Andhra Pradesh decide to get on a train to Amritsar in search of his mission? But that was exactly how he arrived in the city, not knowing the language or the culture. Indeed, it was destiny that he happened to meet my father-in-law, who was looking for someone to take care of their family temple. The rest, as they say, is history. He was the priest at our wedding a few years later and another 25 years later, he also presided over my daughter Ritu's wedding.

This connection, which was instantaneous, lasted almost 40 years till he left this earth. We bonded in many ways as I quizzed him about my life, about my duty as a soldier and as a Brahmin from a priestly family who must understand the scriptures. He was patient and understanding, doing his best to address my existential questions with his in-depth knowledge of the *Ramayana,* the *Mahabharata* and the epic *Bhagwad Gita.* I also delved into the *Guru Granth Sahib* and the Holy Bible to find my answers. Having *Mahatmaji* by my side was deeply reassuring and Amritsar became special for his presence.

For my daughters, the relationship with Amritsar was far more complicated. Having grown up on the stories of this holy city, they deeply respected the legacy of their parents' connection with Amritsar and yet, being daughters of an Army man who had taken them far from their roots, they struggled to fit themselves into this world. It was commonplace for them to grumble and complain about this and that, commenting on how every visit to Amritsar would be etched in their mind and their nostrils.

'What is this smell?'

My girls would ask when a curious mix of fresh cow dung and open drains assailed them with its unfamiliar aroma. They could hardly deny that this was an adventure, much like going back in time to an era that no longer existed. In this walk-through nostalgia, even in the 1970s when electricity was widely used, their large courtyard continued to be cooled by the manually operated traditional *punkhas*.

The toilet on top of the roof still employed the manual scavenging route and so this dry toilet with no sewage, which was cleaned by people, was a difficult transition for my city-bred girls. Fortunately, the switch to the plumbing system finally happened in the late 1970s after much cajoling, but these became one of the many reasons why my daughters dreaded the hometown visits even more.

Even after a slew of modernisation, which resulted in an upgraded lifestyle that incorporated modern features that vastly improved the quality of life, my wife's parental home continued to be a relic of the past. But this was not the real reason why interest gradually dwindled and then completely vanished. Those polite visits that were meant to keep the filial bonds alive were unable to survive indifference and apathy. It was becoming painfully obvious that none of us could move forward from the past.

Then came the sentimental part of the visit when my wife met her father and the girls reunited with their *Nanaji* (mother's father). Whatever the time, he would sit up on his bed to greet each of them while the rest of us stood around the traditional four-poster bed. He would address each girl by name in his loud and authoritative voice and then hand over some money to buy *kulche chole* and *lassi* from the neighbourhood *halwai*. My father-in-law was inevitably dressed in the traditional white kurta pyjama, seated on his pristine white bedsheets, surrounded by old family photos and portraits, making it a walk down memory lane. Urmil often described the joys of her hometown to our daughters and talked in the minutest details about the authentic taste of food, of the real flavour of Punjabi *kadhi* simmering. Another huge plus for Amritsar was the fact that it was and is a foodie haven. For those who wished to soak themselves in the sheer joy of eating, there could be no better place.

Over time, the children loved to savour all those delicacies that Urmil sang praises about. When they were younger, the girls would listen in amusement as she waxed eloquently about the *kulche chole*, the *lassi* and *kulfi falooda,* among other things. It was only once they actually tasted the food that they could agree that, if anything, those descriptions were under-exaggerated. This was the ethos, the culture and the heritage of Amritsar, where everything about the place was extra. The versatility and the deliciousness of its culinary heritage were beyond imagination. And every visit was a foodie haven - from the drool-worthy paneer sandwiches, which were doused in sauces and chutneys and then dipped in gram flour and deep fried to reveal layers of potatoes and cheese to the luscious fruit cream, the ice cream sodas, the *Bheege Kulche*, curd in *donas*, thick *lassi*, *kulche chole* and more.

The bond with this city was also deepened due to the visits to places that were steeped in history. It was always a sombre moment when we visited *Jallianwala Bagh* and a boisterous day when we made a trip to the Wagah border. All of these were nostalgic, but none as much as when we visited *Katra Dulo.* The iconic house and the history behind it were always a bit complex, but it suffices to say that there was some tension and friction.

It was later that my daughter confided in me.

We love the authentic Amritsar life. We know that this is our history and our legacy, and it means something to us. Not only is it my mother's *Mayka*, but it is also our *Nanka*. But it is truly painful to walk the narrow alleys, the stinking gutters and then to see our mother so distressed while communicating with her own father, our *Nanaji*!

I felt the same way even though I had such a good bond with my father-in-law and loved to exchange pleasantries as he pulled out a *beedi* from behind his right ear and offered it to me.

I declined, preferring my Dunhill, which I never lit when my family was around. But I did reach out to offer to light it with my cigarette lighter, which I then gifted to him. The smell of *beedis,* which could normally be nauseating for the girls, acquired a nostalgia of its own and became a part of my own experience. He continued to call me Captain *Sahab* in a rather affectionate gesture even though my rank had changed many times since the time I first met him for the marriage discussions.

Urmil would stay detached through this short meeting and then proceed upstairs to meet the rest of the family, particularly her sister-in-law and the children and her step sisters and brothers. *Pappaji* as he was called, was generous and loving in his own way, but the tension of unresolved issues had created a rift with Urmil and a high level of stress for my wife. And that is why, in just a few hours of being in her childhood home, she was ready to leave.

It was after one such visit that I asked her gently why she could not spend some quality time with her father. This time, she decided to answer this question.

'If we don't learn from past experience, we are bound to repeat history,' she spoke softly, almost as if she couldn't bear to articulate this thought.

'What does that mean, Urmil? What are your concerns? And what do you need to be cautious about?' I asked.

'We are each of us unique individuals who must live life on their own terms and with their own moral and emotional compass. I am committed to my family as long as they fulfil their end of the relationship.'

She refused to divulge anything more, and as always, I didn't want to probe further. Urmil had zealously protected relationships, but not when they interfered with her moral compass, which was unwavering, even with respect to the people she was closest to.

So, I chose to talk to her about her childhood and her family instead. I was relieved to see my wife open up about her tumultuous past, even as she continued picking at the *methi* leaves in an attempt to avoid eye contact while she bared her soul.

'I am the fourth of five siblings born on the day of Holi, barely two years before India got its independence. And yet, I have never really celebrated my birthday or even the festival of Holi, for that matter, because it was never safe for girls to be exposed to anything that involved close contact. As pure Brahmins, pure vegetarians, and very traditional Hindus from Punjab, ours was a family of priests turned businesspeople. The surname we carried was Jaitley, though my father preferred to be called Pandit Balak Nath. My mother, simply known as Rani, must have been an *apsara*, an angel, a beauty because she was described in glowing terms by everyone who knew her. Her mother-in-law, our *dadi,* said that her skin was translucent, and she was kind, sensitive, and affectionate. I just wish she stayed long enough for us to know her.'

I gently squeezed her hand, reminding her that while no one could take the place of her mother, I was there for her. She blinked back the tears and continued.

'All four of us resembled her, but none more than my eldest sister Swarn *Behenji,* who was said to be her replica in looks and in her mothering. She was much older, too, as by the time I came along, *Behenji* was not only married but also expecting her first child. My nephew Manmohan is just a little younger than me, ensuring a special bond, the hallmark of our close-knit family, which consists of my two older sisters, my only brother Kailash and my youngest sister Shama.

She smiled at the recollection of her family's love for each other before she went back to her reminiscences.

'It was my mother who had lovingly named me *Guddi* because she felt I was too light, as weightless as a kite that freely glides in the skies.'

She sighed as if she was imagining floating freely across the horizon.

'Fortunately, I was also given the formal name 'Urmil', which stuck with me, though there is another story of its controversial nature. The character of Urmila from the Ramayana was appreciated for being loyal, trustworthy, committed, and value-driven, but she was left behind by her husband for a period of 14 years even though she begged him to take her along. The fear that I may inherit her qualities as names are very powerful worried me for a long time, but when the time came to marry, I chose to focus on the positives.'

I knew what she was hinting at. Like Urmila, my Urmil had already faced challenging separations, but she was steadfast like a rock, supporting me even when she was physically far from me. She shook me out of this reverie by continuing the story.

'I do not have too many memories of my mother as she was bedridden after my birth and then my youngest sister's arrival a year later became a death knell for her failing health.

We lost her when I was three and then *dadi and nani* - both child widows cared for us.'

'But what about your own father? He was around to support his children, wasn't he?'

I thought of how my father struggled to care for us after my mother's demise.

'*Pappaji* was nothing like your father, even though he had been quite a good father so far. My sisters tell me that he would even walk us to school and back in the early days after mother's death despite being busy with his factory, which manufactured aluminium boxes.

'What changed this situation?

'He changed. We were told that he was heavily influenced by our Uncle, who accompanied him with the specific intent of finding him a new wife. He justified this quick wedding by insisting that he did it for our sake but she herself became a mother very soon, and there were so many, one after the other. As a mother, how could she be expected not to favour her own progeny?'

'But did he at least look out for the four of you?' I persisted.

'Yes, he did, but only for a while. And the excuses were business-related. That he could not afford to spend on us as the factory was going through heavy losses. People began to notice how he changed his dressing sense and began to wear his old, worn-out clothes when his creditors came to the factory or to our home.'

Even though I had heard snatches of similar conversations in hushed whispers when the sisters spoke among themselves, this was the first time Urmil was candidly exposing her father. I tried to focus on the positive aspects.

'Kailash must have been a big support for your father once he joined the family business. Did that not work out well?' I asked

'Kailash toiled day and night to stabilise the factory operations. Unfortunately, his health took a turn for the worse. He needed financial and emotional support during his ailment, but my father avoided getting involved in his treatment. Even after my brother tragically passed away, leaving behind his wife and young children, my father failed to take any responsibility.'

By now, she was visibly distressed as she recounted those painful days when they learnt of Kailash's illness and subsequent demise. I remember those difficult moments when I was away and she cried for days till there were no tears left to shed. It was no wonder that Urmil drifted away from her own father but closer to her siblings.

Years later, when he passed away and I hesitantly shared the news of her father's demise, Urmil grieved privately and moved on from this chapter of her life.

Through all these challenges, her deep love for Amritsar outweighed the disappointment she felt towards her father. But she did keep in touch with her step-siblings and they with her and me and thus, the bonding continued. The stories were truly wonderful but none as touching as that of the history of their family temple. The temple, which had been a part of their family for generations, was handled by *Swami* Sarangdhar Das *Maharaj,* who became our family priest and my mentor for life.

Urmil and I bonded in other ways, too. We had both lost our mothers at an early age. That trauma may have contributed to a detachment and yet we nurtured all filial ties with relatives. Our love for Amritsar remained steady through the years.

It was somewhat harder for our daughters, who had no such connection with their place of birth. In school, our girls inevitably faced a volley of questions that veered around our unusual surname and the fact that they could never really relate to their birthplace. Even when I tried explaining that the surname which I dropped years ago is our real identity as *Kumaria,* one of the highest Brahmin Castes along with *Jaitley, Trikha, Mohla and Jhingan*, their urban education and our inclusive lifestyle did not sit well with this understanding of caste. They also lacked the roots that others talked about with so much passion.

The main reason was the nature of my job. As an Armed Forces Officer from the infantry wing of the Indian Army, I was in a highly operational and specialised role that kept me on my toes. The Infantry battalions' primary mission is to close in and destroy the enemy through close-quarter violent combat in any operation of war. This meant war postings in difficult and inhospitable terrains, border exercises and operations, long separation from families and of course, frequent movement.

Who can think of Amritsar without thinking of the Golden Temple, also known as *Harmandir Sahib* or the *Darbar Sahib?* From the moment one steps into the soothing pool of water at the entrance to the point where one catches a glimpse of those colourful fish, the soft notes of the Gurbani waft soothingly across the serenity of this pool of nectar!

You cannot help but feel the calm and peace as a completely different world unfolds here. A world in which devout boatmen clean the pond in a deeply meditative stage while staring at the glistening and gleaming domes that are reflected in the holy pool of nectar. As devotees wait patiently in long queues to pay their respects to the Guru Granth Sahib, they also enjoy generous helpings of the delicious *kada parshad* served by devout attendants as they make their way out. Devotees can then proceed to the real *prashad* offering - the mouth-watering food from the community kitchen or *langar.*

And when you step outside the Golden Temple, you can **deep dive into the world of shopping as you walk past colourful** stalls that sell everything from the *kadas* (steel bracelets), *wadiyan* (spicy delicacies), *phulkari* (embroidered textiles) and the famed *juttis* (handmade shoes).

If there was any other place we loved as much or even more, it was our family deity at the beautiful *Durgiana* temple. The *Durgiana* temple bridged the gap between the Sikhs and the Hindus and continues to be an example of religious harmony. Said to be a replica of the *Darbar Sahib*, this was another much-loved spot that housed our family deities. Both Urmil's side of the family and mine had immense faith in the power of the temple, more so as my children would love to spot their grandfather, *Bauji's* name on the plaque as he had been a manager and administrator of the temple after retiring from Government service. How could one visit this beautiful temple and not enjoy a hearty *puri-aloo* breakfast?

It was thus inevitable that when Urmil and I managed to save a bit of money and were looking for a house of our own, our decision to build a bungalow on Green Avenue in Amritsar was unanimous. We both agreed that *'Prem'* would be the most suitable name for a house, which would be a tribute to the love we had for each other and for this holy city and remind us of our mother's love.

This beautifully serene home became our summer retreat and we made it a point to make a road trip every year and spend quality time in the house that Urmil and I built. Money was perpetually tight, and we needed to rent it out for the majority of the year, but every time there was a change of tenant, we made sure we used the opportunity to live there. In this way, Prem, my mother, remained an integral part of our life, giving us the physical connect with this city.

Of course, all was not fine, as rumblings of dissent had begun in the early 1980s with a steady rise of extremist forces in Amritsar. This would affect every person who lived in

Amritsar or loved this city deeply.

My beautiful Amritsar began facing the heat when extremism started growing rapidly in Punjab in general and Amritsar in particular. As the calls for *Khalistan* became more strident, we began curtailing our visits to the city and worried about our extended family, who continued to live there.

We had built our dream home in Amritsar, and I planned to settle down there after my retirement. But now, the doubt crept in. Would it be safe for us to live in a city at constant war?

The *Khalistan* Movement, which was essentially a separatist movement seeking a Sikh homeland, gained traction slowly but steadily. It gathered steam under the leadership of Jarnail Singh Bhindranwale in the late seventies and eighties.

Ever since the *Khalistanis* waged serious war against the country, it had shattered so many dreams, creating circumstances where we decided to sell our precious house 'Prem.' We hoped that things would improve, but in the meantime, it made sense to break immediate ties with the city we have forever loved.

In the meantime, the leader of this movement, Jarnail Singh Bhindranwale, became so powerful and exerted such a strong influence on the youth that they responded enthusiastically to his call for a separate nation.

This was also the time that Delhi hosted the Asian Games. Knowing that the Games would receive extensive coverage, Akali leaders overwhelmed Delhi with a flood of protestors, aiming to heighten the perception of Sikh 'plight' among the international audience. Negotiations between the Akali Dal and the Government failed at the last moment due to disagreements regarding the transfer of areas between Punjab and Haryana.

It was being whispered in the inner circles that extremist

forces responsible for bombings and murders were taking shelter in Gurudwaras, yet the Indian Government did not want to hurt Sikh sentiments. It was only after the murder of six bus passengers in October 1983 that emergency rule was imposed in Punjab, which would continue for more than a decade. And when it became clear that the extremists were indeed hiding in the *Darbar Sahib* to escape police action, it was time to do something about it.

It is pertinent to note that *Khalistan* supporters were well trained and when they boldly occupied Amritsar's most sacred and iconic Golden Temple, including the Akal Takht complex, they had a fool-proof plan in place.

For us, there was a kind of suspension of disbelief on hearing news reports that the purity of the Golden Temple was being thus misused. It was particularly disturbing to all those who had love and respect for the city and its heritage.

An Indian summer is legendary. But the summer of 1984 was unforgettable. Radical forces were at work and it was hard not to be affected when your own homeland was threatened. I, who had always been desirous of being in the middle of action whenever an opportunity to defend the nation arose, for once didn't envy the soldiers who entered the holy premises to destroy the enemy within.

What does one do when the nation must be protected from the forces within? Terrorism is even harder to deal with than war with a known enemy – this was a huge realisation for me.

From 3rd to 8th June 1984, a massive operation to regain control over the Harmandir Sahib in Amritsar was ordered by the Prime Minister of India at the time, Indira Gandhi.

Electric supply was cut off and a complete curfew was observed with the Army and para-military forces patrolling

Punjab. Rail, road and air services in Punjab were suspended and foreign entry was completely banned. This was a momentous decision and these were hard times.

Operation Blue Star had two components to it. The first one was Operation Metal, which was confined to the Harmandir Sahib - the Golden Temple complex, followed by Operation Shop, which raided the Punjab countryside. The second component that was launched throughout Punjab was Operation Woodrose, which was carried out by the Indian Army using tanks, artillery, helicopters, armoured vehicles and tear gas.

Harmandir Sahib's not existence were completely sealed and the Army started bombarding the historic Ramgarhia Bunga, the water tank, and other fortified positions. About 100 died in pitched battles. Gurcharan Singh Tohra, former head of SGPC, went to negotiate with Bhindranwale but was unsuccessful.

The BSF and CRPF attacked Hotel Temple View and Brahm Boota Akhara, and by night, both structures were under their control. Army tanks were utilised to destroy the Akal Takht, which did suffer some damage but the structure continued to stand upright. By the afternoon of 10 June, the entire operation was over, with the Indian Army gaining control of the Harmandir Sahib complex.

This was an uneasy time for many reasons because even though Operation Blue Star was successful, it was widely criticised for its no-holds-barred approach.

According to a New York Times article written just a few weeks after the operation, 'Before the raid on the Golden Temple, neither the Government nor anyone else appeared to put much credence in the *Khalistan* movement. Bhindranwale himself said many times that he was not seeking an independent country for Sikhs, merely greater autonomy for Punjab within the Indian Union....'

Celebrated author Khushwant Singh wrote in a similar vein, '*Khalistan* sentiment seems to have arisen since the raid on the temple, which many Sikhs if not most, have taken as a deep offence to their religion and their sensibilities,' referring to the drastic change in community sentiments after the army attack.

Not only did the media in Punjab face a complete blackout, with journalists being denied entry, but Indians working for foreign media were also kept away. The curfew in Punjab was total, and there was literally no transportation across the state.

As part of the Defence Public Relations, it was my job to escort the Government sponsored Doordarshan crew inside the Golden Temple precincts to ensure that the footage was not only accurate but also kind to the government.

This was a harrowing experience for me. As we walked inside my beloved *Darbar Sahab* I was overcome with emotion. Distraught to see my beloved city of Amritsar and its jewel in the crown – the Golden Temple in such shambles, I broke down and begged forgiveness.

That evening as we flew back in the Army helicopter, I wiped my Army boots in vain, trying to rid them of the bloodstains as I muttered, 'Out damned spot,' a famous line from Shakespeare's play, Macbeth. There was no way to wipe off the damage to the temple or the collective psyche of the people of Punjab.

Our brief at the Ministry of Defence was simple - that the media coverage of this operation be done as carefully as possible and that this task be handled maturely by our department. This was a gruesome time for me as Amritsar is my hometown and I belong to the Sikh regiment. What occurred after that was even worse. The assassination of Indira Gandhi, followed by the atrocities against the Sikhs, were moments in history that should never have occurred and I was in the midst of it all.

My mind wandered to the teachings of the Gurus as I recall that Guru Hargobind Sahib pioneered the concept of *Miri-Piri*, with *Miri* signifying temporal powers and *Piri* being the spiritual power. As *a Sant Sipahi,* it was my duty to follow the Guru and practice this learning.

My face was splashed across Doordarshan News on television, and not surprisingly, my wife and children felt a real fear that I could be the target of the extreme forces. As I was visible on screen at a time when tempers ran high.

This fear was heightened when, one night after my appearance on television, there was banging on the main door and a group of Sikhs were visible through the peephole. Even as my daughters begged my wife not to open the door, she asked,

'Kaun hai.' (Who is it?)

The voice on the other side seemed to shudder as they articulated the words *Fauji.* My girls were not convinced, but my courageous wife instantly opened the door to see some of my former soldiers standing outside, distraught because they lost their brother in a road accident.

They had hitched rides to reach the city and having no place to go, came to my house. She did not turn them away. Like a mother, she fed them a hot meal and promised to help them reach the morgue the next morning. She spent most of the night hearing them out as they lamented their loss. I arrived early in the morning and accompanied them to the funeral.

Just months later, Prime Minister Indira Gandhi was assassinated by her Sikh bodyguards, Satwant Singh and Beant Singh, on October 31, 1984, four months after the incident.

Post Indira's assassination, anti-Sikh riots took place and continued for a few days, which killed more than 3,000 Sikhs.

As I look back at those harrowing times, all I recall is that the power of our faith kept us sane even as we did our best to help the innocent Sikh brethren escape the inevitable backlash.

And through all this, it was my lady love, even more than me, who soldiered on.

The song is ended, but the melody lingers on

1990
Gurgaon

Indeed, the Army was my first love. But that was in my heydays, much before Urmil came into my life. Truth be told, it was her presence in my life that completed me, making me indefatigable and resolute. It is this love triangle that I like to call U R Mi Lov.

My wife was a true *Ambarsarni,* born and brought up with love in her maternal home in Amritsar. Even though some of those precious relationships had gotten complicated when her father remarried after her mother's death when she was barely six years of age, there was a strong bond intact.

It was her grandmother and older siblings who showered love and affection on her and her youngest sister, but even that could not make up for the neglect she faced from her father. I knew she hurt, but she avoided speaking about the hurt and pain.

It was not the new family that was the cause of the rift; it was more to do with the unfairness meted out to her older brother, Kailash, that made her drift further and further away till she became distant and aloof from her father.

The final nail in the coffin came when her only brother, our most beloved Kailash, passed away at such a young age.

Urmil's world collapsed. He was not just managing the family business at their factory with Urmil's father but was also the pillar of support for all of them. That he passed away due to an untreated kidney ailment at such a young age was heartrending and just another example of the materialistic nature of her father, who had no qualms in neglecting the family he left behind – Urmil's widowed *Bhabhi* and two young children. Urmil's maternal connections were now limited to her sisters and sister-in-law as all attempts to make her father support her *Bhabhi* were to no avail.

The situation kept getting grimmer, with her father cutting off her late brother's family completely from the family business.

This is when something snapped in Urmil. A strong votary of patience and love, she had a major showdown and walked away from her own father with her head held high. In the years that followed, she kept her vow and even though she cried when she heard of his passing away, she chose not to attend the funeral. Needless to say, she stayed deeply attached to her *Bhabhi* and nephew and niece. I, too, considered them like my own children.

Whenever one hears of family discord and disagreements, the elderly are rarely held accountable. This episode was an eye-opener for me, especially when I heard my spiritual mentor, *Swami* Sarangdhar Dasji, say to Urmil, ' If he does not protect and nurture like a father, he does not deserve your love and respect.'

My own father, too, supported Urmil in one of the most heart-breaking incidents as she decided to forsake him in support of those he had wronged. It was proof of her strength of character that she would not tolerate wrongdoing, no matter who was on the other end. I must admit to being a bit intimidated.

'Would you even discard me if I walked the wrong path,' I asked.

She gave a slow and sad smile as she replied, 'Only if it was something unforgivable.'

I was humbled.

Urmil was truly the epitome of good values and devotion. She truly walked the talk when it came to values. Her loyalty to her marital home was complete as she cared for the home, the staff, my father and me. As life fell into its routine, *Bauji* resumed his own specific morning schedule, which included early morning tea at 5.30 am followed by a long walk, a fixed breakfast of poached eggs on toast and his diary writing.

Urmil was determined to serve her father-in-law to the best of her ability, but she was a pure vegetarian who had never touched onion or garlic, let alone eggs or meat. She could not fathom the technique of poaching eggs by dropping them into hot water and went through trial after trial to get it right. My ever-understanding father decided to drink the water in which the eggs would keep dissolving as he was none the wiser on cooking methodologies and accepted this dissolved format of a poached egg. It was over the weekend that I shared the trick of putting salt or vinegar in the boiling water to ensure that the poaching was complete. In another hilarious episode, we ended up buying just five pieces of *bhindi* (okra/ ladyfinger)to cook for three people under the assumption that two each would suffice for the men and one for her. Seeing the *bhindi* reduced to a mere spoonful alarmed her to no end, so she declared she didn't need lunch at all. Perhaps these are mundane events, but they brought us closer as we navigated family life.

And then there was another time when Urmil's sister, Shanti *Behenji* gifted us a pressure cooker when they visited us while also suggesting that it makes excellent *rajma* (kidney beans). Our attempts to cook in it were met with failure as the beans were completely raw even in the mandated time. Exasperated, we dumped the brand-new cooker under the sink and declared it unworthy of being used. It was only when Shanti *Behenji* visited us and asked us how it worked out that she laughed at our foolishness in not placing the whistle on the cooker. It was then that we realised how it actually worked. What sweet and innocent days these were! We were childlike and open to learning and so it wasn't just about appreciating the magic of a pressure cooker. Urmil and I began to slowly understand the intricacies of cooking and housework with a fresh perspective and soon, there was no looking back, at least for Urmil, as she immersed herself in the process of housekeeping. Thanks to her curiosity and quick intelligence, she began browsing through magazine articles and refined her skills. It took her no time to turn into a gracious hostess and a superb cook. Her organisational skills were equally exemplary and the parties at our home were the talk of the town. My simple Urmil completely immersed herself into the life of an Armed Forces wife.

All was not well on the health front for me. I would fall ill often, and for the most part, I was suffering silently and uncomplainingly. It was a series of different ailments - from kidney stones to stomach ulcers to repeated bouts of food poisoning. Work pressures and poor health became part of my life and in all cases, the doctor's orders were similar. A simple diet, more exercise and less stress. As always, Urmil took the lead in making sure it happened. She put me on a strict food regime, incorporating the right foods. I was a gourmand and a smoker who also enjoyed a drink or two at social events. This time around, I knew she meant business and it was for my good. My wife, being far more practical and real, found the fine balance between good food and health and insisted we go for regular walks. This was also the time that I needed to set a good example for my daughters and so I finally quit smoking and reduced the drink to one or two a month. Our home was joyous and wholesome as soon as this kind of healthy lifestyle returned once again. It was a full house with me, my wife, my father and my three daughters. Not just people but even those four-legged creatures and the birds could find compassion in our home. Our home was a haven for animals – be it the pet dog Ringo or the cat Megha or the birds, rabbits and chickens who were kept in the large outhouses in the sprawling Army homes. Of course, there was a time when we even kept turkeys, cows and even a horse.

I look back fondly at those days, recalling compassion and care, but only because my Urmil was there. Urmil did not restrict herself to housework. An accomplished teacher, she had an interest in stitching, knitting, and cooking. Her love for children and the underprivileged was not lip service. She took service before herself very seriously.

She would sometimes confess her love for the movies, but only if it echoed her values and ethos. Of course, she made an exception with the films of Dev Anand, Waheeda Rehman and Mala Sinha, and enjoyed the movie 'Guide' thoroughly. There was a time early in our life when we struggled to find common ground, as I would rather watch Roman Holiday or Casa Blanca. But our love for each other was far more important than that. We would soon go on to enjoy Bollywood and Hollywood equally.

Music was another leveller. The record player at home was a prized possession for both of us, and those precious records were maintained with precision. Even our daughters loved playing the old numbers and dancing to them. They were quite accustomed to seeing me cajole Urmil into dancing the waltz or foxtrot as I played 'Come September.' Of course, we were a charming couple at the Army parties, but my wife didn't want any of that attention. She was a private person who prioritised family over everything.

In the midst of work and all the typically busy moments, my wife constantly reminded me of my fatherly responsibilities and urged me to find suitable grooms for my daughters. The eldest was barely out of college when we found a perfect match for her. It was in 1985 that my daughter was married to a wonderful young man. The role of my spiritual guru, *Swami* Sarangdhar Dasji, was paramount, as it was with his blessings that we found a suitable groom for our oldest in a match made in heaven. *Kanya daan*, the holy ritual that parents of daughters perform, was done by us and is considered very divine. Today, people do not believe in these customs, but they are key to our culture, not because we objectify women but because we give them the respect they deserve.

It was the best of times and the worst of times, to quote Dickens. Just when we thought it was time to retire, I received my transfer orders. It was challenging, but the time to move had come. I was posted to 22 MCG Sub Area in Guwahati in Assam. The hardest part was uprooting my middle daughter, who had joined Delhi University. We decided to work as a family and prepared ourselves to make a final move to the North East of India. It did not disappoint us. Even though adjusting to a new place at a later stage in life was no easy task, the support of family came in handy. It was here that we received news that my daughter was blessed with a baby boy. And that night, a herd of wild elephants made their way to our house. From our window, we spotted the baby elephant slurping the sap of the banana tree and felt blessed.

The next two years went like a dream. We made frequent trips to Shillong and family life smiled at us once again. Knowing that I would be retiring from Guwahati made it imperative that we make our plans. We had always believed we would settle in our hometown after my retirement but we still had two more unmarried daughters and their future was our first concern. We debated where we should settle on retirement. We decided to buy a home close to Delhi in the upcoming suburb of Noida.

Being an Armed Forces personnel is not just a profession. It is our entire life and so retirement felt impossible. After the most active operational life, it is not easy to hang up your boots. More so for me, as I was hoping to get a job even before I superannuated. But it was not to be.

It was frustrating to be superannuating at the peak of my efficiency and suddenly have nothing to look forward to. But that is how the Armed Forces stay young and agile – by retiring us early and getting fresh blood to take our place.

I retired in April 1989 and recalled how frustrating it was as I felt let down by those who promised me a job, like the editor of The Hindu, who promised me a Defence Correspondent position and did not honour it. I did not let that affect my ambition and relentlessly set out in pursuit of a job. This was not an easy time for me. New home, with all its challenges and a retired life that I was just not ready for. Fortunately, I used the time well.

Sterling Publishers gave me a contract to write two books – Wingate and Japanese Offensive. My trusty Remington typewriter came truly handy as I worked on this mandate and produced two books in 6 months. Those books continue to be prescribed and read in so many of the Armed Forces Training Centers and Libraries across the country. While these were satisfying achievements in their own right, that was a different era altogether. It was difficult to manage on a pension and I desperately craved meaningful work.

Only my eldest daughter was married. We had two more to go. Not many people in today's time would understand that the real challenge in bringing up daughters lies in countering the deeply ingrained mindset of those who continue to believe that girls are a liability and test their ability to adapt to them rather than accept them for the wonderful women that they are.

I have loved being a father to my three girls. Along with my wife, they dominated our household to the extent that I was continuously outnumbered, but I never minded that. Having girls was never the difficult part. Like my own father, I was basically tired of dealing with societal norms that not only belittled our girls but also overlooked the feelings of the parents of the daughters. We were inevitably on the back foot, especially during the early days. It has been ingrained in our culture that our daughters will leave the parental home for their marital home, thus preparing us to detach ourselves and learn to let go. On the other hand, there is an equally ingrained feeling that the boys will not only bring home a bride but also tend to the parents' requirements and be available to them. These are the kinds of social norms that put pressure on young girls and boys and also create harassment for the parents as all forms of emotional domination keep them constantly anxious. Fortunately for us, all our girls found their path over time, relieving us of the tedious tasks of tracking their married lives. As they got on with their lives, sometimes making difficult decisions, we were so proud of their adaptability and strength.

Money was never enough as a retired Government person in those days and neither was time on my side. Just when a sense of frustration began mounting, I was lucky to meet Mr Raj Chawla of Estate News and Views. He saw that hunger in me for work and trusted me with the responsibility of managing his weekly newspaper. I immersed myself into this new world with a vengeance. No job was too small for me and I was determined to prove my worth.

Fortune favours the brave, they say and I can proudly say I am an example of that. When I completed my tenure of over three decades with the Indian Armed Forces, it was easy to rest on my laurels and manage my finances with the pension offered by the Government of India. But I burned with ambition and refused to sit back.

Around this time, my second daughter Meenakshi was married to an Armed Forces Officer and I could now settle into a new life full of changes. My new stint took me to different places as I interviewed top property developers. My biggest coup was my meeting with KP Singh of DLF. It was destiny for sure and the rest, as they say, is history.

I developed an immediate rapport with Mr KP Singh and in no time at all, he trusted me to be a part of a dynamic team that would handle the marketing of their newest township in Gurgaon. After having served in the Army, this was a completely different mandate, but it was a challenge that I seemed to have been preparing for all my life, so I was more than ready to take it on. Within days, I was part of DLF and my work took me to Gurgaon frequently. Since we were living in Noida at the time, the distance became rather inconvenient. So when an opportunity arose to buy a house in Gurgaon, I was ready to sell my bungalow in Amritsar and my flat in Noida to make it happen. It was not an easy decision, but it turned out to be one of the best we made. This is how we shifted to Gurgaon and occupied a beautiful townhouse in the G block of DLF Phase 1. Our new home was a happy place where we made beautiful memories and which our girls and their families visited often.

I loved my work, and Urmil was happy to be at the home of her choice. With ample sunshine and lots of green spaces, it was her dream home. We settled into the neighbourhood and were fortunate to be surrounded by some fine people. With Chand and Kuldeep Rai on our right and the wonderful Mr & Mrs Puri on our left, we were in good company. It was a golden period when our third daughter got married.

This, too, was a match made in heaven, or so we thought. No sooner was this marriage solemnised than it was apparent that it was a mistake. Even our best intentions did not ensure happiness for our daughter and this bothered us. The atmosphere at home was fractured but we remained completely supportive of our daughter. This trying period was a low point but one in which many families suffered, as did we. We learnt to let go of expectations.

Two glorious decades with DLF were the most gratifying period of my life. Finally, my wife and I could enjoy a comfortable lifestyle without worrying about counting the pennies. My loyalty to DLF and its inspirational chairman, KP Singh, was so complete that my wife teased me that DLF meant the world to me. She was somewhat right. I was obsessed with Chairman K.P Singh's vision of Gurgaon emerging as the hub of business and luxury lifestyle. Years later I would be proved right as DLF scaled new heights in providing an enviable life to all those who come in search of better living.

Work was satisfying and DLF grew from strength to strength. From affordable housing to DLF offices to chasing the luxury market to becoming the leader in the super luxury segment, I have seen it all. After over thirty years of dedicated work with DLF, it was time to take a step back once KP Singh handed over the reins to his son. I may have no longer enjoyed the trust and confidence that I had earlier but I knew I still had a lot in me to give back to society. Alas, the government infrastructure left much to be desired but here, too, it is the addition of the right people that can take the public-private partnership model forward. It is the Gurgaon model that encouraged the voice of the citizens and as a result, social activism drove positive developments.

Even though it's been almost ten years since the day my stint with DLF formally ended, I continued to be active and productive by devoting myself fully to the Real Estate Development Organization that I had proudly founded many decades ago. My deep belief that the Real Estate Sector needs ethics was taken well by many and rejected by many more. But I refused to give up. And DLF retained me because, with my contacts and connections, I could continue being the voice of ethics in reality.

My three girls, the '*Teen Deviyan*' who I visualised when I was just married, were now mothers of sons, five in all. I called them my '*Paanch Pandavas*' and Urmil and I love them dearly. For my daughters, their brood takes precedence and those very girls who looked up to me for protection and security advise me on how to run my life. But I am a true soldier and continue to hold tight to my independence and to my ability to make decisions that make sense to me, regardless of whether they make sense to anyone else.

To my mind, real strength goes much beyond physicality. Even in my academy days when I was stout, I could not be taken lightly by anyone because I have always been a risk taker, a maverick if you may and destiny has always sided with me. I have inevitably risen from the ashes. But it was a heavy blow that life gave me and it was not easy to recover from it.

Hamari Adhuri Kahaani

Unfinished Story

2007
The Call

'It is the birthday month!'

I was well known for my theatrics and when I would announce this line dramatically, generally in the beginning of March, depending on when Holi was falling, Urmil would look exasperated.

I loved this game where I wooed her every day, and she shooed me away. But, seriously speaking, anyone who knew me well accepted the special significance of the festival of colours in our household.

Not only did it mean a flurry of impromptu parties where I could get away with my guilty pleasures of ordering both *samosas* and *jalebis*, but it also meant I could go on shopping sprees to flood the house with trinkets that I felt Urmil would love.

Not unexpectedly, she would protest. And I would cajole her. Sometimes, when I chose to romance her in front of people, she would blush and then I would sing '*Na tum hume jaano, na hum tume jaane…*' with all the swag of Dev Anand.

I admired her openly and when I unabashedly announced myself to be the most 'henpecked' husband, she would scowl at me in mock anger. We both knew I was as dedicated to her as she was to me. But that didn't stop the banter.

'How many times do I have to say that I don't want anything for my birthday?'

She would sulk and fume depending on the price or the quality of the gift I bought for her. I was undeterred. My daughters would watch this drama unfold year after year.

The only part I dreaded was when it went overboard. Urmil was sensitive and could quite easily become over-emotional. And then none of my apologies would suffice. I wish I could make her happy all the time, but that was impossible when I was as obsessed with work as I was with her.

Other than these small glitches, we were the best family ever.

I had long accepted the fact that I was a dedicated soldier who loved books as much as the tough Army life. But I also confess that I was most devoted to the women in his life.

Graceful, gracious, a perfect nurturer, I was fortunate to have my wife's unstinted support. It was her generosity of spirit that spelt magic for our family of five. I strived to live up to her expectations of me and even when I did my best to be a generous provider, it was only possible because Urmil was by my side, much like the Goddess *Annapurna* herself. A judicious spender, she spent time budgeting for the least wastage and ensuring that ours was happy and well-kept without being lavish or frivolous in any way.

My memories of Urmil are too many to narrate, but the one story that stands out is our visit to the much revered shrine of *Vaishno Devi* near Jammu just a month before her death. This visit was momentous as it was a true testimony to her faith in the Divine Mother.

It was somewhere in June 2007, just after a grand visit to the National Defence Academy at Khadakvasla near Pune, where my coursemates planned a reunion. After three days of merriment, Urmil and I decided to make a trip to Goa to spend time with Meenakshi. Our middle daughter, also a fan of the Mother, recalled the good old childhood days when we visited the holy *Vaishno Devi* cave in the Himalayas.

As she regaled us with her memories of the challenging climb to the chants of '*Jai Mata Di*' and expressed a desire to relive the experience, Urmil seemed to be absolutely taken by this vision and encouraged her to plan the trip.

'Would we walk all the way to the top?' He asked and Urmil nodded almost instantly.

And that is how a grand plan unfolded, one where we all trekked under the twinkling stars, up, up, upwards towards the mother. All the while, there was another plan unfolding, but little did we know.

The faithfuls believe that the journey to the Holy Shrine of *Mata Vaishno Devi* starts with the Call of *Mata.* Once a person receives it, they are bound to visit the Mother to receive love and blessings. A popular slogan in local folklore beautifully expresses it when they say, *Maa Aap Bulandi*, which means that the Mother Herself Calls!

In fact, while we were planning this trip, friends and well-wishers warned us that since *Navratri* and *Diwali* were the busiest seasons, train reservations would be difficult, if not impossible. Undaunted, the Mother took care of it all. On the day of the journey, we struggled in a traffic jam close to the Old Delhi Railway Station and as the train departure time crept closer, we expressed concern about missing the train. Urmil reassured everyone in her characteristic accepting style that whatever happens is God's will. This refrain of *Mata ka bulawa* guided us at every turn.

After a hearty breakfast at Jammu, we hired a taxi to take us to Katra and back and enjoyed a dream drive with playful monkeys and wooded forests followed by long barren stretches of land. Despite the constant heavy security, we enjoyed the sights and sounds of this beautiful place, with the crisp, cool air a harbinger of our Himalayan trek. It was noon when we arrived at the base camp and enjoyed a pure vegetarian lunch before we began the walk towards Banganga, where the Goddess is believed to have shot an arrow that spouted clear water for her band of monkeys to drink. Our grandsons donned the red glittering scarves that denote the pilgrim's progress and Urmil complimented them on how appropriate they looked as they raced ahead excitedly.

I and Urmil kept each other company at a slow but steady speed. The first hour surprised us with its steepness, and as I touched Urmil's arm, I was alarmed at her cool, clammy skin and panicked, wondering whether she was up to the climb. She reassured me laughingly that she was fine and kept walking.

I, at 70, and Urmil, at 64, led an active lifestyle and though I was concerned about her, imploring her to consider riding a pony or sitting in a *palki*, I also had complete faith in her fitness and we enjoyed this journey together. I indulged as I also regaled her with fun and jokes interspersed with serious spiritual discussions and lots of snack breaks since these were the demands of our grandchildren, who kept the excitement going by moving back and forth between the two groups, their grandparents in one and their parents in the other.

I joked that Urmil was the leader of the weak party while our son-in-law was leading the strong team. It was in this way that I continued to cajole her to lead us with constant motivation...She obligingly egged us on with morale-boosting words even while we laughed and enjoyed every turn and twist that made this a challenging yet fulfilling journey.

At many points in this climb, we enjoyed interacting with fellow pilgrims who smiled and wished us well, impressing us with their devotion. The young girl in her bridal attire with high-heeled shoes in hand hanging on to her husband, and the old man who carried all his belongings on his head and just kept walking, were examples of faith and belief.

I marvelled at the easy manner in which Urmil and I walked hand in hand in a magical evening that gave me time to reflect on the beauty of life, on the importance of cherishing every moment and the good fortune that blessed us to have the love and support of family members. Chants of *Jai Mata Di* provided much needed encouragement.

Vaishno Devi is said to have emerged when her three main manifestations - *Maha Kali*, *Maha Lakshmi* and *Maha Saraswati* pooled their collective spiritual strength. *Dharm* (Righteousness), *Arth* (Material Pursuits), *Kaam* (Contentment) and *Moksh* (Enlightenment) are the four wishes promised to those who visit *Mata Vaishno Devi*.

Our family has never been overly ritualistic and yet we respect and enjoy all the beautiful ceremonies surrounding our faith. Urmil was the guiding light with her practical and committed approach to prayer and worship. She infused discipline and a sense of responsibility that came from a strong value system and from fairness and justice. In spite of these sterling qualities, she was never other-worldly, rigid or predictable. Her sense of humour and bubbling enthusiasm gave us the push to follow our dreams, while her stoicism and faith provided the anchor to maintain harmony and balance with our personal lives.

Even though we looked forward to reaching *Adhkuwari*, we could only stop briefly both because it was too crowded with pilgrims having dinner and also because we longed to reach our destination. We were informed of a new route and were rather excited that it cut the journey by a few kilometres. Amazingly enough, despite numerous warning signs, all six of us completely missed the shortcut we were looking for and found ourselves traversing the long-winded, steep climb known as *Hathi Matha* (the forehead of an elephant).

Urmil and I were at the forefront of this effort and Urmil was extremely triumphant as we reached the end of the steep climb onto the plain surface and proclaimed that we had successfully completed the toughest part of our journey and were now heading for a much easier climb. She looked so happy, so fulfilled and so full of life that I marvelled at her energy. It was as if she was transported to another world. We paused just a little longer while looking at the twinkling lights of *Katra* below and admired the beauty of nature. The Gods seemed to smile at us as we discussed the myths and legends that surround this holy shrine and when the children joined the spiritual discussions, it was truly *satsang.*

As we approached the area known as *Bhawan,* which lodges the holy shrine, our pace quickened. We had booked a family room with six comfortable beds at *Gouri Bhawan*, a short distance away from the main shrine and it was here that we bathed and changed in preparation for a visit to the shrine.

Urmil suggested we rest after *darshan* since it was obvious that the shrine was near and the rows and rows of horses and *palkis* and people just overwhelmed us. It was humanity milling around for salvation. We made our way down the vaults to deposit shoes, watches and mobiles and were inspired by the faith of those who huddled in blankets trying to catch forty winks after completing their *darshan* or perhaps waiting for it.

We soon joined the queue of pilgrims and began the slow but continuous movement towards the sanctum.

As I stood before the Holy *Pindies*, a wave of bliss washed over me. I recall opening my eyes to sense a divine presence. I had to blink twice to check if I was dreaming and all I could see was Urmil bowing her head in reverence.

Those 60 seconds at the shrine revitalised me and as we collected the *Prasad* and the sacred silver coin of the shrine board, which is believed to keep our hearts and pockets satiated, I felt fulfilled.

Our residence for the night was *Gouri Bhawan,* where, in the middle of a restful sleep, I woke to see another divine scene. It was Urmil, the eternal nurturer, adjusting the blankets on her grandchildren, on her daughter, and even on me with a gentleness that was characteristic of her. This selflessly caring gesture to the sounds of the chants wafting from the shrine a few kilometres away is a memory to carry in my heart.

Come dawn and she was the first to awake, arranging tea and biscuits for all of us. By 7 am, we were ready to leave. There was a kind of solemnity in the air as we bid goodbye to the mother, which was in sharp contrast to the bonhomie and exuberance on the way up.

Our train journey from Jammu to Delhi was spent sleeping off the tiredness of the day and when we reached home, it was another reason to celebrate.

It was the day of fasting called *Karwa Chauth,* which Urmil and our daughters observed together for the first time ever. I wanted to join them but was thoroughly admonished by Urmil. Undeterred, I decided to forego breakfast while she looked unhappy at my decision. It was an exciting day full of conversations and music. There was something touching about her concern for her daughters and me when she, too, had spent the whole day without food or water. A woman's heart is truly large, full of the spirit of selfless service, I reflected.

The journey to *Vaishno Devi* gained significance the next month when Urmil's health took a turn for the worse just two weeks after this trip. She complained of a pain in her stomach, which turned so severe that none of the usual medicines worked.

A battery of tests were ordered only to discover the unthinkable. She was diagnosed with cancer in the final stage. This diagnosis of terminal cancer was completely surreal. My mind and body refused to process this information.

Just hearing them say that my darling Urmil had so little time on earth was an out-of-body experience. I felt as if a part of me was dead. After 45 years of closeness, how could she possibly abandon me?

And what was I supposed to do without her?

Would it be possible to carry on when Urmil is gone?

My daughter had to physically stop me from gulping glass after glass of water in a bid to wash out the dry throat that followed this unspeakable prognosis.

The next two weeks flew by at the hospital, where innumerable tests sucked all the energy out of my delicate wife.

And yet, these moments, too, were lightened up by her smile, her decision to apply a red lipstick, by her unwavering faith and her unflinching devotion.

Prayers and hospitals are all I recall of that trying period where I reached out to all the priests I knew, all the temples that I could see and just as swiftly as she entered my life, she was gone. Like *Mata Sita* herself, it was as if the earth just took her back in its fold. An era was over, peacefully for her and harrowingly for me.

I still have no idea how I picked up the threads of my life after her departure. I knew I needed help even to take a few steps outside the house. It was as if my body failed me. For months altogether, I lost my appetite along with a will to live. I, who enjoyed meat and even made my vegetarian wife cook it for me, turned vegetarian in her memory.

Her loss was unbearable, but faith in the powers above was unfailing.

She was, is and always will be my saviour. She was a part of me as long as I was alive, so she will continue to be my guardian angel. I could still talk to her, even if she couldn't reply, because I knew instinctively what her answer would have been. She was my soulmate and my moral compass, urging me to do the right thing. To be selfless, to be present, to be an inspiration. Every special occasion was dedicated to Urmil and even when we visited a restaurant, I would keep the chair next to me vacant in her memory.

Time is indeed a great healer, and as life limped back to normalcy, I learned to cope with this colossal loss. While the grief and the pain never really go away, they take a backseat as time goes by.

If time stood still…then love without pain would be all I know.

— Luke Davies

2020
Mahamari

Winters are definitely getting harsher. Is this the climate change everyone is talking about? I have begun to avoid stepping out of the warmth of my room. Not that there is anywhere to go since the dreaded *Mahamari* funnily named 'Covid 19' reared its ugly head.

I wrap myself in the woollen dressing gown, trying to get comfortable and cosy before returning my daughter's phone call. It will be an effort to sound like my usual self and be answerable.

Of course, this is not an ideal situation. The only person who could legitimately question me was Urmil. I do not wish to give this right to anyone else. As a parent, I must relent and do my best. So, I made that call to allay concerns and to placate her, but something told me it would not be enough.

'*Haan Beta*, I have been busy today.... attending webinars. We are preparing for a big unveiling of our 'Affordable Housing Mission...' When? That is something I cannot say, but I am trying to do this as soon as possible.

Yes, of course, the country is going to reopen soon, I hear myself say, though I do not believe that it is ever likely to go back to what we call normal. I choose not to express my real thoughts.

'As long as you are safe, no problem,' she responds with enthusiasm. 'This webinar sounds super cool, but how are you managing these online sessions on your own?'

I felt it was grossly unfair to underestimate my abilities, but I chose the high ground. What else can one do when your own children doubt your abilities?

'I am well versed in technology and quite comfortable with online sessions. In fact, I will be having my very own session soon and when I do, I will send you the link. I hope you are equally comfortable with the latest technology?'

She was suitably amused by my retort but continued with her list of instructions, which I tuned out.

'I will be waiting to get that message and the link to log in. And please be careful. Wear your mask wherever you go, Papa and make sure the staff is vaccinated.'

I found this tiresome, this need for repetition of the obvious. It reminded me of my coursemate and good friend *Tankha,* who warned me to be wary of daughters becoming overly involved.

'They will begin by mollycoddling and mothering and eventually kill your independence,' he cautioned at a time when I was newly single and a lot more vulnerable.

'Of course, I am careful...but I cannot be imprisoned like this forever,' I protest.

'You are hardly imprisoned, Papa, not when you have this lovely garden,' she responded with a lot more compassion.

'And then there is the unfinished business. I have spent months fine-tuning our plans for 'Affordable Housing'...I cannot leave it incomplete.'

I was exasperated at the hand of fate in my golden years. This mission was my reason for being. The first phase in 2010 was a dream and so perfect was that time that I called it 'Tan-Tana-Tan', denoting the year of 2010. I was all set to surpass my own record when I envisaged the next ten years and termed it 'Dan-Dana-Dan' to refer to 2020.

Alas! Just when our dreams began taking shape, the world was brought to a standstill by a virus. On the cusp of this crucial mission, all offices shut down, as did our work. And with that, my dreams came crashing down.

I reflect on what we all have seen. We belong to the partition generation and have been hardened by those devastating losses. But this is equally if not more unprecedented. What a shame that a pandemic has put a spanner into our plans.

I was shaken out of my thoughts to hear my daughter still in counselling mode.

'The world is at a standstill. Everyone is going through the same problem. Watch some movies, focus on yoga at home....' She continued.

I could not argue any more. It was increasingly difficult to be confined to the house and yet the screaming headlines that dramatised the rising death toll could not be ignored either. It was enough to scare the daylights out of anyone, but I was not just anyone. I decided to end this discussion once and for all.

'The day I stop focusing on my mission will be my last day on earth. I refuse to give up. Never did and never will. I was, am and will be 18 till I die,' I repeated a catchphrase from my days in the 18 Sikh, which I deeply believe in.

She interrupted me gently.

'You are amazing and your life story is simply fascinating. Wouldn't it make for an amazing book?' She asked

'But only if you help me write it,' I said softly as a thought struck me.

She was thoughtful for just a few seconds. And then she responded.

'It is a brilliant idea. You have experiences that need to be shared. Let us utilise this forced 'me' time in your life story. Let's pour all that energy into your 'magnum opus'. Let us finally make your book a reality. That would be the best use of these pandemic times.'

I had a story to tell, and this was the right time to put it all together. We had worked as a team before and whenever we did, it was magic. Or, as a colleague at DLF put it, 'A Force Multiplier.'

'We can start working on it from tomorrow. I will share the link for an online session. At least I know you are adept at it…' She said cheekily as she suggested a format.

Once we agreed on the timings and the call ended, I started scribbling my thoughts almost immediately. They centred on the turbulent times that we find ourselves in. The first paragraph just flowed from my pen.

'I write this at a time when the world deals with wave after wave of a pandemic so wild and sweeping that it is linked to a tsunami that wipes everything in its wake. And while we take all the necessary precautions to dodge this insidious virus, we are unable to wish away its existence. COVID has not just spelt doom for many traditional businesses; it has also given a gloomy outlook to economic recovery, and yet, amidst this unending misery and loss, it has heralded the need for a COVID revolution. This is my Mission for 2021. From the Industrial Revolution of the 18th Century to India's entry into the world stage in the 20th Century with a green revolution and a white revolution to dispel the concerns of 'Roti, Kapda aur Makaan,' it is now a race for vaccines, oxygen and improvements in the health infrastructure. Just as World War II brought an end to the Gold Standard, so also the War against Covid has become the harbinger of sweeping changes that can only be implemented when we overcome the

global divides and boundaries and rise above religion and parochialism. We are now entering a new era where political gains and dishonest dealings that amass wealth unfairly cannot be acceptable. We must create a new system of living and a new thought process. In the wars I fought as a soldier, we were focused on preserving borders and political land. Today, we must preserve our physical and mental health and embrace change if we are to survive this Mahamari called Covid.'

After I shut my laptop, I wondered. Am I destined to see the end of this revolution or even the completion of the final phase of my Affordable Housing mission? It doesn't really matter. As Krishna said in the Bhagavad Gita,

You have a right to *Karma* (actions) but never to any fruits thereof. You should never be motivated by the results of your actions nor be attached to your prescribed activities.

Even in my eighties, I have no plans to slow down or stop till my last breath. I refused to move in with any of my daughters, as I have no plans of being dependent on anyone. Though I myself have happily and respectfully cared for my own father in his old age, I would not want anyone to do it for me. I plan to continue earning and living independently till it's time to hang up my boots.

Even in the past, I have overcome difficult circumstances, but I have never been one to give up and I won't do it now. It was getting late, so I decided to rest and resume writing the story the next day.

That night, I had my most perfect dream. I imagined myself actively serving in the Indian Armed Forces with all the passion and enthusiasm that I could muster. What wonderful years they were, even though I struggled when I began my journey at the National Defence Academy. It was so vivid, the memory that the next morning, I felt a sense of clarity and wrote furiously, sometimes in sentences and sometimes in points.

I am driven by my vision of a better tomorrow. I wish to be true to my mission, to fulfil my reason for being born. I have served my time.

When one door closes, another opens and being a true *Sant Sipahi*, a scholar, a spiritual person and a soldier makes it imperative that I tell this story – the sooner, the better.

I remind myself that I will die with my boots on. I also accept that my time has come!

So long as men can breathe, or eyes can see,
So long lives this, and this gives life to thee.

—William Shakespeare

2021
Epilogue

Dear Papa,

You made Fridays special. It was that simple decision to connect on weekly Zoom meetings for a couple of hours every Friday that changed my life.

I still recall that moment when you said with conviction, 'I want to record my life story for posterity.'

This project, which started in June 2020 and continued right through until March 2021, was more than an activity. It strengthened our bond and was an amazing opportunity for us to converse on so many subjects, turning into the best part of the week.

We laughed, we cried, we joked and we worried about the raging Covid but we never paused, never stopped those weekly calls. Not even when I implored you not to tax yourself while recalling incidents of many decades ago.

You knew that time and tide wait for none and so you delved deeper.

Papa, you have had the most amazing life. While those tales of valour at the war front from 1962 to 1971 are well chronicled, only a few of us knew what a diehard romantic you were. How head over heels in love you were with the woman I called mom.

To see you break down as her lifeless body was lifted from our home to the cremation ground remains my most painful memory and yet, in the months following her early death, I discovered a side of you I had never known.

Determined to be self-reliant and independent, you became a workaholic who wouldn't pause to rest!

In your bid to make us get on with our lives, you immersed yourself into a world of your own.

As you worked and travelled with a vengeance, I see the same stubborn and determined mindset that made you run away from home as a 15-year-old to join the Indian Army because you couldn't bear to live in a home where your mom had died.

Your reminiscences were truly enthralling and I had to work at your speed to keep pace with you. You were a workaholic, I knew that, but that you had such a high sense of duty, and conscientiousness is something I learnt from you.

And even though mother complained that you would not give enough time to the family, she and I admired your energy and work ethos.

So, while I did try, I also knew it was impossible to ask you to take it easy because you were driven like no one I know.

By March 2021, those clouds of gloom were slowly creeping into our weekly calls.

You would blank out some dates and repeat some incidents, but all the while, you were determined and insistent that work on this 'Magnum Opus' should not stop.

And when you just didn't sound right during our weekly

online discussion session, even though the second wave of Covid was raging, double-masked, I arrived late in the night.

It was almost midnight when the taxi pulled up in front of our house, which was brightly lit up with bright lights, lulling me into believing all was well.

As always, I didn't have the necessary change to pay the taxi driver, so I walked into the house to ask you for some change. I stopped in my tracks to see an elderly man, a far cry from my youthful and energetic dad, painstakingly counting notes and loose coins for me.

What happened to you, Papa? I wondered. Wasn't it just one year ago that I met you?

In barely 12 months of isolation, you seemed to have changed. And even though you made a real effort to keep that air of optimism around you, I worried for you. I got a fleeting glimpse of my grandfather, of *Bauji,* from way back in 1978 when he would have been the same age. I brushed the thoughts away and met you enthusiastically.

It was overwhelming to see you continue to keep up the fatherly concern just the way you always did. You kept reminding me that there was dinner kept for me. And even when I politely declined, you still kept insisting I eat.

I felt uneasy, as if there was something that I needed to be afraid of.

As we inched closer to midnight, your trusted attendant Abdul and his wife, Saheeda - the in-house cook, asked me if I needed anything. They both looked worn out after a long day. I, on the other hand, was wide awake, and as I craved time with you, I asked them to retire for the night.

I decided to sleep next to you. Wiping tears and muffling my crying, I lay next to you, awake in the dark, very conscious of your deep sighs as you uttered *Shri Ram kripa kare* again and again. Your faith inspires me even today.

'We will visit the doctor first thing in the morning,' I said to you as much to myself while praying fervently to all the Gods and made all attempts to keep myself calm.

I wondered how it was possible that in spite of weekly Google Meet calls and all those regular conversations with us, your daughters, you were able to sound happy and healthy.

There was the moment of truth, the realisation that this pandemic doesn't just claim lives by infecting the public but also by isolating them. All those months of being huddled away in honest attempts to keep our parents safe, we barely realised how lack of socialisation and regular health check-ups could affect just as fatally as the infection itself.

And when it comes to someone like you, who is so intellectually curious and full of a sense of adventure, I should have known that hours and hours of webinars and Zoom meets would never make up for a real connection. Even those lazy chit-chats with the in-house staff clearly did not keep loneliness or poor health at bay.

It must also have something to do with your temperament. A soldier could not be caged, especially one who would never complain nor admit to any ailment as he found it a weakness.

I was assailed by a sense of impending doom and I couldn't help but feel a wave of regret!

Why did you not agree to move in with us when we repeatedly invited you?

Why did you not call for help?

Why would you never ever admit to deteriorating health?

And why was it that whenever we asked, 'How are you, Papa?' it would be met with your classic reply - A cheery 'First Class!'

I have always been a fan of your courage, your consistency, your sense of independence, and your 'never give up' spirit. It was all the inspiration I needed. But now things were different and so when I placed my hand over yours, reassuring you that I was there for you, I was so emotional when you squeezed my hand back.

Seconds later, you called out to your attendant, Abdul. You would rather have him next to you.

I conceded and peace prevailed. The next morning, you were unusually enthusiastic, acting as if nothing was wrong at all.

' I want to get ready for the doctor's visit…I need to shave and bathe,' you demanded and asked Abdul to lay out his clothes and help him shave.

Abdul smiled indulgently and whispered to me that he hadn't seen his 'Sir' display this much energy in a long time.

And after that long bath, you emerged fresh, fragrant and cheerful, all ready to go.

I smiled to see you. Your bald pate glistened and your face glowed.

'Don't I look like *Dandi Swami*?' you asked.

I nodded and smiled and we set off for the clinic.

The infection in your feet was significantly present and seemed to have gotten worse, but you were determined to walk. You even pulled yourself painstakingly up the long length of stairs to visit your doctor. As we arrived at the clinic, we were joined by my sister and brother-in-law, your eldest daughter and son-in-law.

The doctor had one look at the swelling on your feet and scribbled hurriedly on her pad. She was concerned and referred us to the closest hospital.

While your resilience continues to be inspiring, we were now aware that this was an emergency and that there was an alarming deterioration.

You seemed unfazed, even triumphant, as we made our way home.

'I could see that the doctor was impressed to see me looking so clean - like the original *Yogi* that I am.'

I smiled at how fiercely independent and strong you continued to be.

The very next morning, we were both seated at the OPD, but one glance from the nurse was enough to send us to the ICU of Max Hospital in Gurgaon.

'Possible Sepsis,' the attending doctor said while mentioning that it was treatable.

I heaved a sigh of relief as the treatment began, especially since you were so cooperative and understanding.

I was joined by my elder sister and brother-in-law, and within a day, you were moved into the room with the doctor pronouncing you well enough to leave the very next day.

We tried to be normal and while you enjoyed your breakfast, asking me for more fruit, more custard, and more attention, I tried to keep that nagging worry at bay and watched you lapping up all that attention.

Even the doctors and the staff got a rare glimpse of just how amazing a person you could be. Not just that, two days later, you seemed to have made a miraculous recovery.

We headed back home in your car and as you sat next to me, you admitted, 'This is like a dream - so unreal, I am here watching everything, but it doesn't feel real.'

'You will be fine, Papa. Must be all those medicines.' I assured you, wondering what was going on.

Soon, it was time for me to leave and while you seemed to be looking better, you asked me to stay a bit longer, even telling me how much you needed me. I wish I had heeded your words, I wish I had stayed back, but I rushed back to my husband and kids.

I promised you I would be back soon and instructed his attendant on how to care for you, but sadly, it took an emergency to bring me back.

You insisted you wanted to see me off, but then you turned and went into the toilet. My cab waited outside and the clock ticked.

'Papa, can I leave?' I called out

'I will be out soon…wait for me', you said calmly

Another few minutes and I knew I would miss that flight. Suddenly, you stepped out and walked me to the door as if nothing at all had transpired.

I felt overwhelmed with love and instinctively turned around and kissed you on the cheek in a most unusual gesture that surprised and pleased you and me.

At that very moment, you asked Abdul to click a picture of us together as we stood next to each other at the entrance of the door of your home. It felt like a goodbye for some reason and I recall that I had to repeatedly wipe tears in the cab. A few weeks later, you would once again ask Abdul to click a photo, this time with your *Fauji* grandson as you saluted him.

My next trip came a couple of months later, on hearing that you were admitted to the ICU once again, I was hoping to spend more time with you at home, but it was not possible.

You were propped up in ICU with oxygen being given off and on and yet you recognised me. You were still paying attention and that made me feel optimistic.

From that moment onwards, my sister, me and you held hands and prayed on your favourite *Hanuman Chalisa.* As I would say in one stanza, you would sometimes mumble and, at other times, clearly recite lines, refusing to give up or give in.

It was mid-July when we began seeing you fade away as you drifted in and out of consciousness with moments of clarity followed by delirium. True to your Army background, your hallucinations activated your soldierly side and you worried for your country - that the enemy had taken over. You pointed to all the nurses and attendants milling around your bed in the ICU and exclaimed…

'They want to destroy us, Meenu, they want to take over the country ....look at them congregating and plotting. They are the MI 6… Do not let our country down.'

You were so convincing and so articulate that I had to hold your hand and reassure you.

'No, Papa, they are friendly. They are our own people. They love us...You are a brave soldier and you are safe. All is well.'

You calmed down. Your light brown eyes twinkled, but you had a vacant look.

My wise father, you were a child again, so innocent and so untouched, filled with a sense of wonderment. You were purity personified, and when our eyes met, we mirrored and reflected on each other in an undying legacy of love and bravery. A **single tear drop slid down your cheek.**

'Are you in pain, Papa?' I asked gently.

You shook your head vehemently in denial as I, too, blinked

back my tears.

My fear of losing you melted away and I was enveloped in the rarest bond of love. At that moment, my mother's words echoed in my ears when I asked her why she shed a tear when she was in the hospital and my husband came to greet her.

'Why do you cry, Mama? Are you in pain?'

'Not crying because of pain, but because of love…' she had said, wiping away the tears.

Then, as now, the circle of love was complete.

The anticipatory grief that builds up days before the loss occurs melts away when one is face-to-face with that moment of truth. Suddenly, it becomes easier to say goodbye. We lost you a few days later.

Your precious red Ford Figo car was parked in the basement, so when my husband asked me if I wanted to accompany my father or drive the car, I whispered 'Papa' and he walked with me to the morgue in the basement. Soon, the ambulance arrived and we took you home, Papa. To your *Ashram*

As the ambulance pulled out of *Medanta* and drove on the highway, I couldn't help but look at the well-developed city of Gurgaon that you, my dear father, always boasted about. The one that DLF built with your active involvement. You made them and us so proud then and now.

'Death be not proud,' I whispered as I recalled your fascination for attending a funeral, a *chautha,* an *Uthala* or a *Tehervin.*

You felt that attending a post-death ritual is a reminder of how transitory and fragile our lives are.

'When you attend an event like this, it is as if you are the one who died, so imagine you are listening to your own eulogy,' you would say.

Your advice was so sound when you said, 'Support people when they are down. Whether you attend a happy occasion or not, make sure you are with them when they are down and out.'

On another such occasion, when your dearest coursemate and friend Bheesham passed away and was cremated at the Army crematorium at Brar Square, you told me this is what you wanted for yourself. You reiterated that wish to be cremated with military honours at the Brar Square Crematorium with your beloved regiment, The Sikh, in attendance. To see you hold a smart salute in the blazing June sun made me proud to be your daughter, but the next minute, I was rattled when you asked me to ensure you also get a soldierly send-off when the time comes. This ease with which you speak of mortality gives me the confidence to face life and death with courage and peace. I spent quality time with you that day as we talked long and deep about life and death.

This desire unfolded exactly as you wished. When we bid you goodbye at the peak of the second wave of COVID-19, it was your regiment that carried you with honour and dignity, while *Didi* and I, your Army Daughters, felt proud to be *Colonel Sahab Di Kudiyaan* (Daughters of Colonel).

Once again, we imbibed the rare culture and ethos that create such a warm and loving community while encouraging independence and strength.

I realised later that you even put this in your last will.

Both my mother and you embraced death with courage and wisdom, and you inspire us to do the same when our time comes.

Mummy was cremated by Papa, and you were cremated with battle honours by your daughters, with your beloved Sikh regiment in the forefront.

As my elder sister and I conducted the last rites, we felt the very strength that you, as parents, displayed all their lives. And this is why the goodbye was so magical.

You have often narrated the story of how you dreamt of being a father to three daughters even before you were married, making me imagine you to be some kind of a soothsayer who knows the future and maybe that is why even though you couldn't be with us when we were born, you named each of us after your favourite 'goddesses' and we somehow turned out exactly like the names we were given!

A soldier is trained to be brave and courageous in the face of challenges and dangers. But what they manage to do despite their packed schedules and beyond the call of duty is to raise their children with the same military ethos, courage and dignity!

I believe there is a special place in heaven for every Soldier and not just because they live and die with the same courage but because they somehow manage to impart this courage and tenacity to their families as well. And because most of them refuse to discriminate between sons and daughters, it gives them the confidence and courage to conduct the last rites. As my older sister and I lit the funeral pyre and conducted the last rites for you dad, we were secure in the knowledge that you would approve and applaud.

Papa, I remember you saying, 'All the world is a stage and we are merely actors playing our part.' How well you played so many parts and donned so many hats with the same aplomb. Intelligent and resourceful, you were a dreamer, your head forever in the clouds. Yes, you were too much into your thoughts, but you were always strong, brave, and steadfast – a true warrior.

Rest in Peace, Soldier! While we 'Soldier On' till we meet again!